17 STORIES OF DEATH & DESIRE

Andrew Lyall

Copyright © 2022 Andrew Lyall All rights reserved

The characters and events portrayed in this book are fictitious. Any similarity to real persons, living or dead, is coincidental and not intended by the author.

No part of this book may be reproduced, or stored in a retrieval system, or transmitted in any form or by any means, electronic, mechanical, photocopying, recording, or otherwise, without express written permission of the publisher.

An earlier version of *Crowthorne* was originally published in *Local Haunts: A Horrortube Anthology* edited by R Saint Claire

An earlier version *of Orpheus Descends* was published in *Served Cold: A Horrortube Anthology* edited by R Saint Claire and Steve Donoghue

An earlier version of *Auld Aggie* was first published in *We're Not Home: A Horror Anthology* edited by Cam Wolfe

An earlier version of *Upon Returning Home From The Great War* was first published *in Strange Abrasions: Thirteen Untold Horrors* edited by Andy Murray

Contents

CROWTHORNE 7

THE REST IS PIECES 28

AFTER THE MINOTAUR 43

OCTOPUS 57

NOCTURIA 66

ONE HEART 93

AULD AGGIE 108

THE KICKABOUT 125

THE DEATH OF DESIRE 131

THE LAPWING'S DECREE 140

ESAU AND EMIL 156

THE MEMORY OF BONES 165

ORPHEUS DESCENDS 182

THE SHADES OF MIDWINTER 207

IN THE SHADOW OF THE TSUNAMI 210

UPON RETURNING HOME FROM THE GREAT WAR
.... 224

17 STOREYS OF DEATH & DESIRE 233

ACKNOWLEDGEMENTS 251

CROWTHORNE

Crowthorne had been on my mind for some time, so I wasn't surprised to find I'd been drifting closer towards the village I'd known as a girl. The notion that I could go back began as an idle daydream, but once the thought took root it became inevitable that I would return to those childhood haunts of mine.

I don't think I've ever properly spoken about the place to anyone from outside. If you mention something like the carnival, where a young girl is chosen to be the Carnival Princess, and a procession of floats and costumed people move through the village towards the fete on the recreation ground, you can see people conjuring images of *The Wicker Man* or *Midsommar*. But in truth growing up in a village like that was the same merry-go-round that all children are familiar with: school and home, family, and friends, worrying about being popular, trying to fit in.

We did have the surrounding woodland, which I suppose not everyone gets when they're growing up. I've spent so much time since then in bricked-up places that the built-up world became normal to me, but some of us kids had the woods on our doorsteps. We could leave the house, cross the street, and run into the green. We'd hear tell of older boys and girls taking their bikes out after dark and cycling the Devil's Highway, and of course we found evidence of their fires and under-age drinking whenever we played there in the daytime. But we were children, and our concerns were childish. The High Street didn't hold much appeal (save the sweet shops and the video store), but out among the trees we built dens; we hollered; chased; screamed.

It was August and the chill of autumn hadn't quite started to bite, but even so Crowthorne High Street was leaden and grey on the day I returned. I looked down that stretch of road with a queasy feeling brought on by the uneasy mashing of the unfamiliar new and the recognisable old. I hadn't visited Crowthorne for a little over 34 years, and as I made my way down the street again, feeling obtrusively out of place, I was surprised by how many of the shops from my time still survived. They stood like implacable artefacts, and I marveled that these small, niche businesses were still around. They also made me feel increasingly self-conscious. What was I doing here? Everything had moved on. I had moved on. Yet here were these shop fronts dotted up and down, stubborn remainders from decades ago that felt as if they'd been waiting all this time for me to come home.

I caught my reflection in a shop window and half expected to see the pale image of the little girl I once was. Instead, I looked like a ghost out of time, as if my spirit were trapped on the other side of the pane while the other shoppers passed me by without a glance. What would I do if someone called out my name? If someone recognized me? I quickened my pace. I wanted to get off the High Street. I hadn't come back for this anyway. This wasn't Crowthorne, not my Crowthorne. Now that I was here, I wanted to see Amy's house.

Amy Dooley was my best friend. When I think of Crowthorne I think of her. I wasn't returning to the village; I was coming back to her. People called us "the sisters" and eventually, secretly, we agreed that we *were* sisters. She was shorter and slighter, but in my mind's eye she was always bigger than me. She had more confidence and presence than I could ever muster. I was simply happy to follow her lead; wherever she wanted to go and whatever she wanted to do was always fine with me.

Climbing the hill to her house brought back memories of us returning home from school. I was getting a little out of breath but remembered how we used to fly up that hill in our buckled shoes, knee-high white socks, and acrylic navy skirts after the final bell. I thought about Mrs Dooley with a tray of jam sandwiches and orange juice for the two of us – "her girls" she sometimes called us – insisting that we eat something before we both inevitably scrambled outside again.

It wasn't the same when I got to her house. The curtains of her bedroom window were different; an extension had been added to the side of the house;

there was a new front door. It made me feel sad and angry, but what did I expect? Strangers lived there now. Then I remembered Mrs Dooley crying; that strange, strangled noise she'd made.

I don't want to talk about that.

I ran then, along the path between two houses which led into the moist cold of Napier Woods. The muddy tracks were hardened with frost, but I left the well-trodden pathways and stole into a crunching carpet of dead, curled leaves.

The air was thicker here, damp. It insulated me from the outside world. The sounds of my breath and the fall of my feet joined the quiet cacophony all around me – a shiver of bushes to my left as something fled from my footsteps; the chirping whistles of starlings and thrushes in the trees; the overhead "shush" of the canopy of leaves, set in motion by a breeze which didn't quite reach the ground.

How many times had Amy and I run down this path and through these woods? How many of our games had I forgotten? Not the raucous, shrieking hide-and-seek in gangs, or that game of kiss chase suggested by a boy who lived in Amy's street, but the games we'd made up together in our own little world. The pacts we'd made as secret sisters. The things we'd promised never to tell anybody. How much of that was lost to me now?

My heart was racing so I slowed my breathing just like my doctor had showed me. The treetops shimmered and the smaller limbs waved with an easy languor I didn't share. I thought of the interconnected roots beneath my feet and realized with a calming wave that the green understood time differently to us. Unlike the High Street, Napier Woods still felt familiar and welcoming. I wasn't out of place or out of time here, and for these trees my decades away were just a yesterday, and my yesterdays were all still here, waiting.

I remembered the time Amy found a circle of mushrooms, a fairy ring. As I counted my breaths and slowed my heartbeat my lips spread into a smile at the image of her spinning in that circle. She'd twirled and said hello to the invisible fairy folk who were watching from the shrubs and bushes. I joined her, and at her instruction we curtsied to the king who lived beneath the large tree near that fairy ring. We returned to that tree so often it became our tree, "the tree" as we soon called it.

I caught a flash of yellow up ahead on the path, a dog walker's raincoat, and ducked behind the nearest trunk. They hadn't seen me, and they were moving away. Their black dog marked me, however. It paused, extended its neck, and swiveled its ears towards me, but after a moment's consideration it turned and followed its owner.

I waited for a while, minding my breathing, before moving deeper into the woods. I wanted to find our tree. Now that I was back within this mossy, damp air I could recall it perfectly: the thick roots like a hand splayed on the ground, its fingers digging into the earth; gnarled bark with an old man's beard of moss and creeping ivy; that first, lowest branch curving down toward the ground as if waiting to scoop you up, inviting you to climb.

With it so fixed in my mind I was sure that I could find the tree again without any bother, but each time I thought it was near – just around the next turn or over the next small rise – my memories proved false. My steps became clompy and impatient, sturdy boots snapping twigs and kicking up plumes of leaf litter. More than once I turned around and doubled back.

Hadn't there been a song? Something for the Fairy King? Something Amy had made up to beseech permission to approach the tree? Everywhere looked familiar but the tree was nowhere. I got the notion that the birdsong was laughter. Laughter directed at me. I had the mad thought that the tree was toying with me. I mean, it had been magic, hadn't it?

What I mean to say is, Amy and I thought it was magic.

We pretended it was magic.

This wasn't right. It should have been here. I set my steps up the incline towards Broadmoor Hospital even though I knew Amy and I had never played near the high, red brick walls of that place. As children we'd only had vague notions of it being a "bad place". What I understand now as a high security psychiatric hospital filled our imaginations back then with notions of the "criminally insane", those two words conjuring bogeymen in our young minds.

We never went near, but we all lived with the sirens. Thirteen of them, built to alert the people of Crowthorne and the surrounding area if ever one of the patients escaped. They were tested every Monday morning at 10am – a two-minute escape siren which slowly wound down to be replaced by the two-minute all clear tone. It was just part of life in Crowthorne. To outsiders I understand that sounds quite bizarre, but you can find videos on YouTube of the things being tested if you don't believe me.

There was a story, I don't know if it's true, of the sirens being tested one morning and they forgot to sound the "all clear". We heard that a little old lady had locked herself indoors for three days because she thought a patient had escaped. I don't know, we thought it was funny at the time.

Another time an older girl told Amy and I about the "Yorkshire Ripper" who was locked up in there. That was enough for us to keep our distance, trust me. I think maybe I had some nightmares around that same time. My bedroom overlooked our back garden, and even though I didn't really know who the Yorkshire Ripper was back then there were a few nights when I dreamt that he was in our garden looking up at my bedroom window.

How had that song of Amy's gone? It was one of the sing-songy tunes she was always humming distractedly to herself.

Right then a strong image came unbidden of her red wellington boots skipping away from me through the undergrowth, with me trailing, always happy to follow where she led. Those boots danced towards the tree as she sung her song, skipping uphill. It hit me so suddenly that I thought for a moment I was following her again. And then there was the tree right in front of me. It looked exactly as I'd remembered it. I stopped in my tracks and for the life of me I thought I would hear Amy's song drifting up into the branches. For a moment it was strange not to see her sitting on that low branch, swinging her legs, and chattering away.

This was closer to Broadmoor than I ever remembered us coming, but here the tree stood. I drew nearer with my arm out, gingerly, the same way someone might approach a horse. I lay my palm against the cold, scratchy bark and began searching all around the base, thinking that surely after all this time... but remarkably it was still there.

I could just make out the top of the frame amongst the usual woodland detritus, behind the ivy: the fairy door we'd nailed to the trunk between two fat knuckles of root. I dropped to my knees and pulled the ivy away, scooping handfuls of dead leaves and twigs from between the roots. The fairy door was weathered and time-worn, set crooked against the bark and held with bent nails where our small hands had hammered it into place. The door had been Amy's idea, but I knew where my father kept his tools, so I'd brought the hammer and nails to fix it in place.

This was the Fairy King's home. Amy would always address him formally and I know that sometimes she wrote things on notes; wishes and secrets which she slipped behind the miniature doorway. Other times we'd leave bits of food, a corner of a chocolate bar or crisp crumbs from the bottom of a packet. One time we left a piece of Amy's birthday cake for the King.

Now those tiny hinges were stiff with rust and the wood was warped, but adult hands can be forceful and insistent. I wriggled my fingertips into the gap and pulled. I thought I might snap the tiny door off, but with a couple of sharp tugs it creaked away from the tree. I lowered my head to the ground, but there was only the dirty candy floss of a long-abandoned spider's web behind the door now. A woodlouse scuttled out and into the nearby shelter of some dead leaves.

Above the door was more chainmail ivy which I ripped away, noting how the pattern of vines remained in the moss underneath like an X-ray of arteries and veins. We'd carved our spells here in the trunk: our names, some spiral shapes, and stars. There had been a penknife in my father's toolbox which we'd used. They'd been so bright when we carved them, but now they were dark and green, almost indiscernible. I traced our names with a fingertip as if they were braille and then followed one of the spirals to its centre.

This was Crowthorne. This was where we had run and laughed and made our silly pledges to the Fairy King, but this was not the secret place. This was not the Green House. This was where we first played with Mr Twiggs, but soon after that we would all go to the Green House, and eventually I learned that Amy used to go to the Green House alone to play with Mr Twiggs.

Later that summer Amy Dooley disappeared.

Mrs Dooley had cried and made that strange noise in her throat which sounded like the Broadmoor sirens.

After that it was nothing but questions for a long time. People came to my house and sat with my parents and me. Other times Dad would take me to visit the police station to talk about Amy. I wasn't in trouble, they kept telling me that I wasn't in trouble, but I was scared, nonetheless. Sometimes Mum or Dad would come to my room and talk to me gently. They would ask me the same questions as the police.

One evening, after I'd gone to bed, Mrs Dooley came to the house. I heard her downstairs asking to speak with me, getting louder. I didn't want my parents to let her up to my room.

"I just want to know where my baby is," she kept saying. "She must have said something. She must be able to tell me something." But Amy hadn't come to call for me that day, the day she went missing. I told lots of different people again and again, and my Mum repeated it now, down in our hallway with Mrs Dooley crying at the front door.

"Amy didn't come here," she said. "I was here all afternoon myself; I would have known."

"She told me she was going out to play," Mrs Dooley said. "She said that, and we both know that meant she was coming here. They were inseparable."

"She didn't. I'm sorry. I'm so, so sorry, but she didn't come here."

Eventually I told them about Mr Twiggs. I had to, even though it was one of our secrets.

I told the police that we played with him in the woods and then in the Green House, and then I told them how Amy started playing with Mr Twiggs on her own. Their questions went round and round. Sometimes they would take me out to the woods to show them where we played. I showed them the tree. I showed them our tree and felt the stab of my betrayal as I watched these grown-ups set a ring of tape around it and go rooting on their knees through the leaves and dirt with their fingertips. They took pictures. They took pictures of the fairy door and of our carvings, our spells. Then they asked me over and over about Mr Twiggs and the Green House.

I told them what I could.

I told them that I didn't know how to get to the Green House even though they asked me all the time. They asked me to describe it. Was it a long way from the tree? Did you walk there? Did he take you in a car? Was there anything about the place that stuck in your mind? What colour was the door? Were there any tall buildings nearby? Any road signs you noticed? Did it have a distinctive smell?

They asked me to describe Mr Twiggs. They asked me about the games we'd played there. One of them even brought me paper and colouring pencils and asked me to draw him. I made them a picture of Amy and me and Mr Twiggs together in the Green House, but I was never any good at drawing. They seemed disappointed with everything I told them and eventually I got used to the forced smiles and being told I was doing very well while knowing that I wasn't telling them what they wanted to hear. I even sang them one of Amy's songs:

"In the wood,
A little man stood,
Playing in the Green House,
Yeah! Yeah! Yeah!"

We'd sing that all the time, getting louder each time, spinning around until we were dizzy and would fall to the ground laughing. Then we'd get up and do it again, jabbing at the words, heads awhirl, twirling till we must have look frenzied. Trying to walk in straight lines and stumbling, falling, shuffling on all fours like tots, trying to catch our breath while the rhyme still spun in our heads:

"In the wood,
A little man stood,
Playing in the Green House,
Yeah! Yeah! Yeah!"

Thinking back to that made my head spin again. It was fortunate that I was already down on my knees and leaning against the trunk because the blood suddenly left my head and dark flowers bloomed in my vision. Ink blots. Everything around me went fuzzy and a high-pitched whine filled my ears. The blotchy sunlight through the leaves became abstract patterns of pulsing black, white, and green. The tone in my ears was the screaming of the tree and I comprehended that when a tree screams its cry lasts for years. I realized that if I died on this spot and was allowed to decompose into the compost beneath me, I would become a part of that scream.

My vision returned and the whine in my ears subsided. I rolled gracelessly onto my front and pushed myself up onto wobbly legs. A robin sat on the lowest branch of the tree; its bead-black eye regarded me from a tilted head. My mind was a tumble of words like the association exercises I used to do with my doctor: robin, bobbin, robbing, gobbling, goblin.

This time, though, the string of words was in Amy's voice. It was time to move on.

My childish drawing of Mr Twiggs is probably still in an old police file somewhere along with cassette tapes of my interviews. Recordings of my wavering, high-pitched voice cracking and afraid, trying to explain as best I could.

"Secret sisters."

I can still hear us saying that in unison. We said it a lot, linking our little fingers in a promise. I can also still hear me breaking a promise – telling a secret – a small voice in a small room with a policewoman: "One afternoon Amy found me in the woods playing with Mr Twiggs."

After that, their questions wriggled like fingers at a stubborn lock. They pried me open and winkled more and more out of me.

It was the school holidays, I'd said. One afternoon Amy found me by the tree playing with Mr Twiggs. Soon we both went to the woods to play with him and then later we used to go to the Green House together. I found out that Amy had started playing with Mr Twiggs alone in the Green House. I promised not to tell.

They wanted to know everything.

Mr Twiggs lived in the woods, I told them. He would only come out if Amy and I were there. He had long fingers like twigs and a smelly coat of moss and feathers. We went to the Green House together. It was a special place that only we knew about; our secret place where the walls were green. It was damp and cold and there were no lights, so you needed torches. There was an old cot bed with rusty springs, and we could make as much noise as we liked because no one could hear us when we were there.

We moved away that winter, but my parents didn't stop taking me to talk to people. In my head it seems like an endless procession of men and women who wanted to talk to me about how I was feeling, what I was thinking, what I was dreaming about. But I knew they all really wanted to talk about Mr Twiggs. Oh, they'd act friendly, and we'd talk about anything or nothing or whatever was on my mind, but eventually they'd come sidling up to the questions they really wanted to ask. Some of them would wait for weeks but always, eventually, in some roundabout way, they would bend their questions towards him.

Eventually I stopped talking about him, and soon after that – after we'd moved a couple more times – I stopped talking about Crowthorne altogether. If people never knew, I reasoned, they could never ask.

But I would think of him.

I never really made any new friends in any of the new schools I moved to. I missed Amy, of course, in a way words can't describe, but after a while, when I wanted to conjure a friend, more often than not it was Mr Twiggs I thought of and not her. I used to talk to him out loud at first and looking back that's probably why Mum and Dad had me talking to so many people even after we'd moved away. So, we learned to keep our games secret. He'd hide from the adults to make me giggle. He'd be amongst the bushes in our back garden when I was playing outside. He'd be peeping out through the slit in a postbox when we walked past. Other times he'd be angry at me for leaving him in Crowthorne.

I cried for a little while by the tree and then tried to clean myself up as best I could. I made my way out of the woods and returned on shaky legs to the High Street. I was suddenly very hungry and remembered a nice-looking coffee shop I'd spotted which hadn't been there in my day. So, I sat at a table away from the window, had coffee and cake, and watched the late afternoon darken outside.

After that I walked the streets some more, keeping my head down, just measuring out time until nightfall. I had to wait for dark before I went back to the Green House.

That was the one secret I'd kept. The one promise to Amy that I never broke.

"No matter what," she'd said, our pinky fingers locked. "This is our secret place. No one can ever know about it."

"No matter what," I echoed. "I'll never tell."

It was getting cold. I thought of killing time in a pub but didn't want to stick out as an unfamiliar face, or even worse, be recognized. Instead, I walked in varying loops around the quieter streets, always circling back towards the Green House like water around a drain.

I never told anyone where it was, and after Amy disappeared, I never went back there in case I was being watched. That's why I felt sick standing in the dark, closer to the Green House than I'd been for the best part of my life. That's why part of me wanted to leave all over again, because after Amy left me, I had left him, left Crowthorne, and I didn't know if he'd still be there waiting for me. I didn't know if he'd still be angry.

"He's Mr Twiggs and he dances jigs,

In an overcoat like a smelly goat,

And his fingers snap like a crackerjack,

While he spins you round in the underground."

I was singing another one of our songs under my breath, trying to delay the inevitable. It was dark now and quiet enough. No more waiting. No more delays.

The Green House was so close to a busy road that I'd spent every day of that summer waiting for them to find it. Every time the police took me out into the woods, I felt sure they were going to take me there and make me break my final promise.

I crept a little way up the Devil's Highway, past the hum of an electrical substation, and slipped into the wooded area there. This was how Amy and I had always approached the Green House. The trees blocked the headlights and deadened the Doppler hiss of the occasional passing car. Still, I moved in darkness, not wanting to risk the torch on my phone being seen. Progress through the undergrowth was clumsy and each noise I made seemed amplified in the quiet of the night. Something fussed and flapped in a nearby tree and every footstep seemed to crunch or snap something.

As a child the Green House had been a wonderful, secret hideaway. As an adult I learnt it was a Royal Observer Corps Monitoring Post. One of over a thousand all over the country, mostly abandoned now, built during the Cold War to report in the event of a nuclear burst over British soil.

The way in had been overgrown when we were kids and the past three decades had only worked to hide it further. Even in the low light, though – even covered in nettles and vegetation – I recognized the squat, metre high concrete entrance to the underground room.

It took time, and I worked methodically and patiently to reduce any noise, but eventually I cleared enough undergrowth to get to the rusted metal hatch. It took more time and effort to finally lever the hatch open. Stale air plumed over me from out of the shaft, like a puff of mushroom spores, and I stared into the square, black hole. My eyes had grown accustomed to the gloom, and I could make out the top of the iron ladder on one side of the shaft which led four or five metres down into what Amy and I had called the Green House.

I tested the top rung with a boot before committing my full weight to the ladder. A dull creak echoed around the chamber beneath me and with one last look around I swung myself over the edge and began to descend.

Once I was in the shaft my breathing sounded loud, reflecting off the close walls. I could smell the rust on the ice-cold rungs. After a few metres I expected to feel the concrete floor but each time I dropped my foot there was always one more rung. The thought of descending forever flitted through my mind, but I eventually reached the bottom.

I looked back up the stain-streaked shaft and the opening above looked smaller than I'd anticipated, just a square of darkish blue with a whisp of cloud. The world was a creaking climb away.

I could feel the space behind me. It smelt earthy. He was here. He'd been waiting all this time.

I turned slowly. Little pins of light flashed in my eyes — my vision trying to compensate in the pitch black — and I could hear a shallow breathing from the shadows (or was it just the echo of my own breath coming back at me?).

"Mr Twiggs?"

I fumbled in my pocket for my phone, squinting against the screen's glow as I turned on the torch. Sudden light caused shadows to rear and slide around the rectangular room as I swung my arm back and forth. Swirling particles filled the air, caught in the beam like underwater footage of a shipwreck. Part of the far ceiling had collapsed inwards, and roots and mould had got in and spread like a sickness. I could see the corroded springs of the cot at the far end behind the dirty, waist-high cabinet which still stood against the left-hand wall. And there, perched on top of the cabinet, Mr Twiggs was watching me through the gloom.

My shaking hand made his shadow wobble.

"I'm sorry I left you," I said in a voice which sounded louder in that confined place than I'd intended.

He sat, impassive, and for long beats of time I didn't believe that he was actually there. My little stick man. My little poppet made of twigs and leaves, old doll's clothes, and feathers. Bound by string; bound in part by lengths of my own hair. My idea. Mine.

One afternoon Amy found me in the woods playing with Mr Twiggs. After that she wanted to play with him too. She decided that Mr Twiggs should live in the woods, and I'd agreed, happy to play along and follow her lead. So, we hid him in the bushes near the tree and we'd go and play with him together.

I crossed the room and picked him up. His coat was mouldy now, the stuffing was gone, and I could feel the two bundles of twigs tied into a cross which made up his thin body and outstretched arms. He still had his neckerchief on, a piece of patterned cloth I'd taken from an old dress I'd outgrown.

Once Amy found the Green House we started playing there instead, and she determined that Mr Twiggs should move. So, we moved him. And for a while we played with him there. Together.

I looked across at the mouldering cot. Amy was where I had left her.

It's funny, in my mind she's always that little bit bigger than me, but she really was very small on those corroded, bent springs. She'd become shrunken and grey. Her skin looked like old paper, pulled in at the cheeks and eyes, and her fingers looked like they'd snap just like Mr Twiggs' did.

"You shouldn't have played with him without me," I said.

Amy hadn't called for me that afternoon. She'd gone to the Green House without me. It had been easy enough to slip out of the house without my mother noticing. I could still see the handle of my father's screwdriver poking out just under Amy's armpit.

"He was my friend first."

THE REST IS PIECES

Resurrection, when it came, was something like drowning in reverse. A muffled upwards rush. Scrabbling through earth and sod until his fingers broke the surface like foraging grubs.

For a long time after that he floundered: an upturned turtle, his arms and legs paddling back and forth in the soil. His fingers raked at the grass and dirt in silence until eventually he sat, and then struggled to stand.

Once up, he staggered a few paces away from the ragged hole he'd made then bent double, leaning heavily on a rough headstone. As he flopped forwards, head like a ragdoll, clods of mud fell from his mouth while a fat worm slid from one nostril. It hung there for some seconds, curling in the night air before dropping to the ground. There were others way back in his papery sinuses. He could feel them squirming blindly, and when he lurched upright again some of them fell into the back of his dry, raspy throat.

The baleful moon pulsed and glowed and he gazed with foggy eyes, unblinking, at the first light they had seen for… well, time no longer seemed to mean anything. He may have stood transfixed by soft moonlight for a moment or a year. That spell passed, though, once he felt the tug; a pull in his chest as if he were snagged by an invisible fishing line.

He took a faltering step.

The solid sound his shoe made on dry grass dragged him back to the here and now.

There were other shapes moving about in the graveyard, flailing half out of the ground, shambling among the tombstones or floating away in twos and threes like bits of drift ice caught in an unseen current.

That snag pulled at him again. Newer lights. Nearer lights. Brighter than the moon but splintered and cast wide across the landscape below which gently dipped away from him.

Down there. Somewhere. He remembered.

Barbara.

Her oval face pinched with concern as honey-coloured hair fell about it. His wife at her vigil. How long had he been here? Tubes and scans and surgeries? Sometimes it felt as if he were looking up at her from inside a long tunnel, but right now he was present.

Barbara.

The afternoon light of summer was arrowing diagonal into the room, picking out motes of dust in the air and making the tiny hairs on her forearms glow. A white room.

Green curtains. The sky through the window was a slice of cornflower blue at the edge of his vision.

Sometimes she would talk to him, read from a book or the day's newspaper or relay news from the life he'd been cut adrift from. He often floated in and out, unable to catch hold of the words which fell in a garble like marbles from her mouth. But her constant soothing tone was the real message: I love you. I'm here. We're together.

Barbara.

Other times, like now, she was quiet, always holding his hand, returning any pressure he was able to give. He squeezed now and the lines at her eyes relaxed for a moment before creasing a little differently into a smile.

He'd been in an accident. He'd been driving, on his way to meet her, very important that they meet. There had been an unholy squeal of twisting metal – the sound of a person's world coming apart – a giant boar's screech of rusting pain as everything flipped with a jarring crunch. He didn't know how long ago that had been, but the sound stayed with him. He still heard it every now and then on the edge of sleep, or a few seconds after the chemical cold of another anaesthetic spread quickly up his arm. The rest was pieces, flashes, but that noise still came at him out of the dark, ambushing from the depths like a car wreck shark strike.

Barbara was talking and he watched the movement of her mouth as she formed the words, not really absorbing what she was saying. It felt as if her words and the streaming sunlight were the same, washing over him and warming him.

She'd been biting at a piece of skin on her bottom lip. She lifted a hand from his and pushed her hair back behind one ear.

The first thing he clearly remembered after the crash was a nurse leaning over him. He was on his back, hadn't yet tried to move, and her owl face filled his field of vision. She looked directly into his eyes, and in that naked act of looking, of being seen, he realised that he was still here.

"Welcome back to the land of the living," she'd said.

Barbara.

She was down there somewhere among the shattered glass of lights and noise.

There were more of them around him now, those others. They were moving towards the lights themselves in jerky, determined movements. Each of them, he saw, had a fishing line embedded in them – heads, chests, stomachs – gossamer beams of light reeling them in, pulling them forwards. He knew who was on the other end of his line.

He took another step and flailed his arms in counterbalance. Then another. And with each planted foot he became a little steadier, a little surer.

He followed the general stream of the others – with them but not of them – all caught in the same tow. He never thought to look back and learn his own name from the gravestone he was leaving behind. It had already been forgotten.

Coming down off the hill was a struggle with gravity. Figures around him would stumble and fall occasionally; they would roll into others and flap on the ground like birds with broken wings. He lost his footing a few times, genuflecting before rising. With each jolt of a step more mud would drop from his legs, his shoulders, his hair. The dirt which clogged his ears fell loose and he could hear the low choir of murmurs and moans around him. Beyond that the distant noise of traffic and city nightlife was a constant hiss, like waves on a shell beach.

There were plenty still behind him, but by no means was he among the first of the returned. He could see their dotted shapes below fanning out ahead of him like ants across a picnic blanket. Each was following their own invisible imperative, moving through the nearby industrial plant towards the noise and lights beyond.

He had to reach Barbara. It was important that they meet. That call throbbed inside of him now in lieu of a pulse. He needed to close the gap between them. She was waiting at home behind a red door. He could picture it, could remember walking up the path towards it a thousand times, holding his key out. In reverie he reached his arm out now, a pretend key pinched between thumb and forefinger. Home.

Barbara.

The other side of town.

He had to meet Barbara.

Her name became his heartbeat.

He moved into the tall shadows of the silent industrial plant stacks. They'd been wound down and stood unused, a dinosaur graveyard of manufacturing. Grass, shrubs, and ivy pushed through cracks in the concrete and curled over the brick and rust. An echoing clatter sounded from somewhere deeper inside and there were always the soft shuffling feet of the others around him. From up ahead came the screech of some surprised nocturnal animal, a cat or raccoon perhaps. The first scream of the night.

Barbara.

Their first morning together. Her arm across his chest. Her head on his shoulder. She sighed a little and pulled herself in closer, one leg seeking a space between his, and he shifted so that they could entwine. He enjoyed the weight of her on his ribcage. He was almost at peace.

The curtains were thin. Early morning washed the bedroom in cloudy lemonade light. He passed his eyes over her crooked arm, determined to take in every detail as the dark and hectic memories of the previous night hummed in his head. The light brown freckle on her bicep. The curve of her shoulder. The feel of her breast pressed at his side. How much had they drunk to have fallen together like this after how many years? It had been like freefalling. Abandon.

Time was plastic in this moment between sleep and waking. He thought that if he didn't move then he might hold the day in abeyance for a little longer. They might hang in the dawn glow, their lazy, languid limbs slowly coming to life amongst each other. The fizzing, urgent memories of the night would be easily recalled, but this calm, these elegant moments, would dissipate as a dream does if he did not commit them now.

The depth of her breathing changed as she began to wake. He turned slightly, their legs rubbing together, and slid an arm out and around her. He pulled her in and she let herself be drawn. She exhaled unhurriedly, both their heads resting on one pillow now. He studied her face in the brief splinter of time before she opened her eyes, then she was looking at him.

She rubbed an eye with a small fist then raised her head slightly to see where she was. She lifted the covers a little to confirm what she suspected — they were both naked — and then she dropped her head back onto the pillow. A wonky smile spread across her face.

"Morning," she said matter-of-factly. Then they both started to giggle.

A couple of blocks over he heard the first firecracker pops of gunfire. Three quick shots then two more spaced out. There was shouting, the sound of glass breaking.

He kept to the shadows and tried wherever possible to move through the alleyways and backstreets. The dumpsters behind these low rent shops offered good cover, but the waste strewn passages were narrow. There was a fire somewhere and the cramped spaces between brick buildings quickly filled up with sooty smoke. Shapes loomed out of that hot fog. Someone with a rag over their face sprinted towards him, running from some unseen fright, and barrelled straight into him. They fell together, a tangle of limbs. The runner shrieked and kicked out at him with both legs as if they could not stop running. Frantic, ill-judged strikes shook his chest and sent his head snapping back, but there was no pain. Then the runner was up and gone, consumed by the next black-grey billow which rolled over them, flecked and lit from inside by sparks of hot ash fireflies.

Later he had to clamber ungainly over a bundle of two or three of those others who were blocking his path. They were kneeling, hunched, and pawing at something on the ground beneath them. He wasn't sure if it was still making sounds or whether their slick, questing hands were pushing air through a recently dead voice box. Or perhaps now nothing could die.

Barbara sighed.

The air left her throat as if she were deflating.

"Okay, let's try this," she said, "what did you have for breakfast this morning?"

"You know what I had for breakfast."

"Don't be a smartass. Play along."

"Okaaay," he said, drawing out the word and feigning a struggle to remember. "Breakfast, breakfast, breakfast, let me see. I believe I had coffee and a bagel."

"And you chose that of your own free will?"

"Well sure, I chose it."

"Out of thin air?"

"Out of a desire for coffee and bagels."

"Ah!" She sat forwards on the couch like Archimedes in the bathtub. "And where did this desire come from?"

"I like bagels."

"But out of all the possibilities, including skipping breakfast"

"The very thought."

"Including skipping breakfast," she persisted, "which you'd already unconsciously discarded because the factors like time and hunger had already had their say. You think that you chose bagels completely freely, without impediment, a free and fair choice, but you didn't. For a start there were only so many things in the house you could have chosen from."

"I could have gone to the store."

"Nuh-uh, time and hunger had already ruled that out for you. And the reason there was a small choice in the house is because you'd previously picked from a much wider selection at the store; and those choices were driven by previous experience and positive reinforcement; beliefs; upbringing; affluence."

"Farting?"

"You're not funny, you know that, right? I'm serious: if you're poor, say, that will have a direct effect on what you buy for breakfast, or even if you have breakfast."

"So, you're saying I didn't choose to have bagels? The bagels chose me?"

"I'm saying you were always going to have bagels this morning."

"I am funny, by the way."

"We all agree on cause and effect in the physical world. If you kick a ball then physics can predict how far it will go, how fast, what parabola it will express."

"You're sexy when you use big words, but a person isn't a ball. You can't predict what I'm going to do next."

"For starters, whatever you're thinking of doing next, don't. And besides, there is a school of philosophy which says your mind is exactly like a ball, it's just moved by myriad more forces and influences, all much more subtle; some internal, others external, societal, which ultimately kick you in one direction or another all throughout the day. That's hard determinism. Free will is an illusion."

"I sure don't feel like a robot."

"Does a robot? Your mind state is directly tied to your brain state, and your brain state is a physical state. Way more complicated than the ball but still subject to cause and effect. Anyway, like I say, it's just one school of thought."

He mulled this over.

"So, basically," he said, "you're admitting that you had no choice but to fall in love with me?"

She sighed again, mock exasperation, and settled back into the couch and her books.

"And that if I were to tickle you right now..."

"No."

"...It wouldn't be my fault? After all, I was always going to tickle you."

"Don't you dare! Don't you DARE!"

Her last word ascended into a shriek as he lunged.

There were sirens all over now. Mechanical wolf song.

The baseball bat came down again, rocking him, breaking his collarbone. Four of them surrounded him while dozens more were running about the intersection all around them.

Meet Barbara one more time.

He tried to move on, but the loose circle was always with him. One of them kicked him in the back. They were cheering. Hollering.

"Tough old bastard," the batter said. Gunfire was sounding all around now. The bat came down again, across his shoulders this time. The batter was breathing heavily. Another of them swung a fist at his jaw and there was a pop of knuckles as he connected with exposed bone. The puncher spun away, crying out in pain, holding his hand to his chest.

"Bust my fucking hand!"

"You're gonna need shots, you dumb fuck. Lookit his skin, man. You probably got all sorts of hepatitis now."

Meet Barbara.

He lurched towards the hole which had formed in their circle, but the others danced around and closed him in again; their sport wasn't over.

"Batter up!"

The car rounded the corner at speed, clipping the sidewalk in a squeal of tyres. It barrelled through their loose group like they were tenpins then lost control and careened into some parked cars on the far side of the street. The front end crumpled as metal scraped on metal. The driver's side window cracked into a spiderweb mosaic, hit by something dark and red inside which bubbled down the glass. The engine was still gunning, running hot, but something inside was broken and it sounded like the strangled bellow of a dying rhino.

Their five scattered bodies were all motionless for a time.

He was on his back. Hadn't yet tried to move.

The pale full moon seemed to loom over him, filling his field of vision.

The nurse with the owl face was there as well, standing by his side, looking down at him. She said nothing, but her silent gaze denuded him.

The tug.

Meet Barbara.

He sat up reflexively.

The nurse was not there.

The engine whine hit a higher register of complaint.

The pulverised shape inside the crashed car was shuddering. Its stiff fingers scraped over the crumpled dashboard which had pinned it to the seat and practically cut it in half. It would never be able to get out, but it felt its own tug nonetheless, so those dead fingers scrabbled ceaselessly at the door, the steering wheel, the window.

The two parts of his broken collar bone ground together as he pushed himself up from the gritty tarmac. The car's impact had twisted his hip around, but he managed to stay upright. He could stay mobile and keep moving forwards if he shuffled both feet on the floor, sliding them forwards one at a time as if he were walking on an icy path.

The other four, his attackers, who had been flung by the car began to twitch.

As he moved away they began to get up. They stood and dispersed wordlessly, without a glance or a thought for him or one another anymore.

Barbara's face floated in front of him. She was talking and he watched the movement of her mouth, but he could not make out the words, just the constant sound of twisting, grinding metal.

Just meet Barbara.

He reached out a beseeching hand but her face bobbed away.

Honey-coloured hair fell about it.

He grabbed at air like a child chasing bubbles, trying to snag a handful.

There had been shouts and screams all around him for what seemed like a very long time, but they had receded now. They were behind him with the city on fire. Now his head was filled with the tinnitus trill of shattering glass, that keening moment just past the tensile limit, looped over and over.

It felt as if he were looking up at her from inside a long tunnel.

With each shuffling step towards her she floated backwards. Then, in the same way that clouds cover the moon, her face disappeared.

A moment of disorientation.

He looked about him and in the darkness of night the surrounding greens looked purple and blue. He was alone in a park. Paths threaded through the place, lit like glittering twine, but he was in the middle of a large open space and the stars above him exploded across the sky.

An unholy squeal of twisting metal – the sound of a person's world coming apart.

He knew this place. It was near home. He and Barbara used to come here. He'd said something to her once when they were here. He couldn't remember what it was, but he remembered her eyes beading with tears (happy or sad, he couldn't recall). The rest was pieces. Flashes. Whatever memory had been there was like a reflection on a pond, in reaching for it he'd splashed it apart.

How long had he been here?

Just meet Barbara.

He'd been in an accident.

Barbara meet.

One foot, then the next.

And now he was standing on the sidewalk, looking up the path to his front door. Red door.

He could remember walking up the path to that door so many times, but never what came after. There were no lights on in the house. He heard breaking glass but couldn't tell if it was nearby or in his head.

Lazy, languid limbs slowly came to life.

Forwards. Up the path. The red door looked black in the moonlight. All the streetlights were out. He held his arm straight, an imaginary key pinched between two fingers. Barbara was inside. She was waiting for him.

His wife at her vigil.

Just meet Barbara meet.

He was standing in the kitchen now. It was much cooler inside, and quieter. He had never stood in a room without the sound of his own breathing. He felt displaced and wondered if he was really there. The creaking of a floorboard above sounded explosive in the silence. The sound dragged him back to the here and now. He pitched and scuffed his way through to the hall and the base of the stairs. A mountain to climb.

There was a deep cracking sound somewhere around his pelvis as he swung one leg up and onto the first step, then he allowed himself to slump forwards and began clawing at the carpeted stairs above, pulling himself up just as he'd heaved himself out of the ground.

Meet.

Meet.

He cast his arms out when he finally entered the bedroom. He was smiling. He'd been smiling wide this whole time, both rows of teeth all visible.

Whatever you're thinking of doing next, don't.

She was rising; she had something in her hands. He couldn't understand what she was saying.

Meet. Meet. Just meat. Meat.

She rushed forwards.

Meat. *He squeezed now and the lines at her eyes relaxed for a moment.* Meat. Meat. Meat. *"Don't you dare! Don't you DARE!"* Meat. Meat. *Her oval face pinched.* Meat. Meat. Just meat. *She lifted a hand from his and pushed.* Meat. Meat. Meat. *Her last word ascended into a shriek.* Meat. Meat. Meat. Meat. Meat. *Pulling her in.* Meat. Meat. *Her crooked arm.* Meat. Meat. *With a jarring crunch.* Meat. *The air left her throat as if she were deflating.* Meat. Meat. Meat. *Biting at a piece of skin on her bottom lip.* Meat. Meat. *The sound of a person.* Meat. *Coming apart.* MEAT. MEAT. MEAT. *Dropped her head back onto the pillow.* MEAT. MEAT. MEAT. MEAT. MEAT. *The rest was pieces.*

AFTER THE MINOTAUR

A message from his dead husband sent Anton out into the streets during the last night of carnival. He'd finally started packing some of Matteo's things away when a card fell from the pages of a book. It felt so instantly and completely as if Matteo was there that Anton almost called out to him.

Matteo's handwriting looked exquisite in black ink on thick red card:

> *Go to the Piazza di Euridice.*
> *The devil there has your next clue.*

Matteo had loved treasure hunts. It was how he had proposed to Anton, crafting a string of clues which led him around Edinburgh, eventually ending at the restaurant where they'd had their first date. Matteo had been waiting with a group of their closest friends, champagne, and a ring. Birthday gifts and valentines were often to be found at the end of such a trail. They'd been married four years when Matteo got the chance to return to Italy – a position at the university of Naples Federico II – and there the tradition dwindled then stopped. Until Matteo fell sick.

He got ill quickly, seemed to rally for a while, but then began a slow decline which mystified his doctors. During that time Anton nursed and cared for him and Matteo began crafting treasure hunts again; modest affairs with clues written on index cards which would send Anton from room to room, usually ending with a love note.

This card fell from the pages of one of Matteo's thick, scholarly tomes, *The Heart of the Labyrinth: The Maze in Myth and Materiality*. It must have been part of a hunt Matteo had been planning before his illness had taken hold.

The thrill of discovery and the sudden feeling of Matteo nearby was instantly followed by a lancing grief. With Matteo gone Anton now shared his life with this metamorphosing beast. At first his grief had been a bull, charging ceaselessly around the confines of their small apartment, but with time it had evolved and become more precise in the ways it inflicted its pain. Now it pierced him all over and the sounds of the revels outside rose as if the crowd was cheering its thrusts.

*Go to the Piazza di Euridice.
The devil there has your next clue.*

Anton clutched the card to his chest and rose from the mess around him. He pulled on his coat and shoes, rushed downstairs, and ran out into the whirl and madness of carnival.

The streets were busy but not thronging as he joined the steady stream of masked faces. People in costume were moving towards the city centre; some were singing, others dancing. He could hear distant drums and the wasp-like drone of plastic horns, and somebody nearby was playing the fiddle. A warm breeze blew from the east; it came off Mount Vesuvius, tinged with sulphur, and seemed to make the people giddy.

The Piazza di Euridice was only a kilometre away, up a steady incline, and by the time he reached it the crowds had swollen. The noise of their shouting, singing and laughter bounced off the walls of the packed square. Anton was jostled and poked, overwhelmed by noisy blasts of perfume and sweat. Someone dressed as a bear with cowbells slung around their neck lurched past him, led on a chain by a Harlequin. A quartet of ladies in gaudy opera gowns and lace parasols surrounded him briefly, their faces hidden behind pouting porcelain masks. There were peacock feathers and face paint; gold trim and sequined gloves; broad hats and jangling jester caps.

He felt foolish for joining them. He'd been chasing the ghost of an emotion and now his way back was blocked by this maddening surge of people. He felt disconnected from them on a profound level and his grief hugged him like a heavy fur rug. Matteo had planned for him to come here many months ago. Now he was dead. There was no next clue and no path to follow.

A figure caught his attention; it moved easily through the mob, making its way towards the old church at the far end of the piazza. The figure was swaddled in a golden cloak and as it reached the steps of the church it turned and looked directly at him. This person was wearing a traditional devil's mask: red face, black forked beard and small red horns protruding from his forehead. They locked eyes for a moment, then this devil stole past the church doors and slipped – unseen by all but Anton – through an unassuming entrance at the side of the building. Without pausing to question the urge Anton pushed his way through the crowd to follow.

The devil there has your next clue.

Anton was not a spiritual man, he had never ruminated the ineffable, but he chased this coincidence now as if it were the fluttering tatters of something important which was being pulled from his grasp. The clamouring rabble cheered their approval as he slipped down the side of the church and passed quickly through the anonymous wooden door there.

The noise from outside was instantly muted and Anton found himself in a small, dark room, cluttered with stacks of musty prayer books, broken wooden pews, and faded, damaged statues of the saints. He followed the sound of receding footsteps down a small corridor to a stone spiral staircase which coiled down into darkness.

He paused at the top step; he knew this was absurd, but he also knew that if he returned meekly to his apartment then he would spend the rest of his life wondering about this strange serendipity. So, he descended and soon couldn't see the uneven steps in front of him; he only had the rope handrail in his right hand to guide him. He wondered if some of the mania of carnival had infected him as he pressed on. Soon, though, the faintest copper burnish of candlelight crept around the curved stone wall from below.

He stepped out into a low-ceilinged, crypt-like room where the figure he had pursued stood, with his back to him, lighting the thick candles which were dotted around the place. For one weird moment Anton expected his husband to turn, mask in hand, and yell "Surprise!" But at the sound of his footsteps the devil turned and revealed himself to be a man in his fifties, grey beard flecked with white. It wasn't Matteo. Of course.

"Che ci fai qui?" the devil said in a sonorous voice.

"Oh, I'm sorry," Anton stammered. "I thought…" he deflated.

"English?" the devil asked.

"Scottish."

"You are lost?"

"I was looking for…" Maybe he was lost.

His eyes were becoming accustomed to the soft candlelight and he noticed that this man was holding an envelope in his gloved hand.

"I might be going mad," he said, pointing at the envelope, "but I think that is for me."

"It is the right night for madness," the devil replied softly, "but I can assure you this is not for you. This is for one of the poor souls lost here. A name, from a dream, to aid their ascension from Purgatory." Anton's scalp began to tingle. For the first time since his husband's death he felt the syringe tendrils of his grief retreat a little from the chambers of his heart.

"The name," he whispered; "is it Matteo?"

The candles fluttered from some subterranean wind.

Even in these deep shadows he saw a flicker of surprise light the devil's eyes.

"Why have you come here?" he asked.

"I received," Anton struggled to know how to explain, "a sign, I suppose you might call it. It sounds silly, I know."

"Not at all," the devil demurred gently. "I believe that when we intervene on behalf of the souls of the departed a bridge is formed. We try to help them, and they in turn want to aid us in our endeavours. But I believe they can only communicate through impulses; dreams; coincidence; by showing us briefly the hidden pattern beneath all things. The night has brought you here, now, and I think that perhaps you should come with me. My name is Angelo."

Anton introduced himself in a slight daze. Angelo took up a candle and Anton followed him as he made his way into one of the tunnels which branched off from this cellar room. As they made their way deeper into the network beneath Naples, Angelo explained what he was doing down here.

"The underside of Napoli is a web of chambers, tunnels and catacombs. This ground has been excavated since the time of the Greeks and Romans of Neapolis. You can still find their aqueducts, markets and roads down here. You can also find the vast congregation of lost souls we are visiting tonight."

The way was winding, and Angelo soon relied upon a torch he had brought rather than the weak light of their candles. It was warm down here and he explained that the heat came from the volcano. He said that the yellow volcanic rock of this area had been quarried for centuries to build the city.

"And these spaces below," he said with hushed reverence, "emptied to birth the city above. They are the wombs of Napoli."

Anton's mind spun with a mild buzz. An hour ago, he'd been sitting on the floor of his apartment sorting through Matteo's books, but down here that felt like another time. It seemed as if they'd been walking for hours, and he realised that he would never be able to retrace the paths and turns which would lead him back above ground on his own. Angelo told him that they were forty metres beneath street level, but there were times when he was sure that he could hear the jamboree of carnival echoing from distant tunnels. All he could do was follow, and eventually a sort of dissociation took over; his mind became foggy and he accompanied this man as if he were sleepwalking, until eventually Angelo touched his shoulder lightly and said, "We are here."

They had to stoop to enter, and once inside Angelo began lighting the clusters of candles which had previously been placed in niches, on ledges, and in corners of this hollow space. As the warm light grew Anton saw the carefully arranged piles of bones and skulls which filled this place. They were in an ossuary.

"Victims of the plague of 1656," Angelo said, sotto voce. "Thousands buried anonymously in shallow pits; they are the poor who could not afford a proper burial and whose souls languish even now."

He moved with purpose towards a set of skulls which had been separated from the masses. These had been set in discrete alcoves, placed on cushions and adorned with flowers, rosaries, and small trinkets. Angelo took a lace handkerchief from his pocket and began tenderly cleaning one of these skulls. He motioned for Anton to approach.

"We pray for them," he said. "We adopt them, care for them, and we believe that through our intercession their souls may be released from Purgatory. And occasionally," he said, lifting the envelope he had been carrying, "their names are revealed to us in dreams and we can petition God directly on their behalf."

Anton felt woozy in the rippling light, surrounded by these ancient bones and staring into the sockets of the skull before him. He felt certain that Angelo's card bore Matteo's name, and even though this skull was not his husband's, it brought back vivid memories of Matteo's gaunt face at the end; of skin stretched thin over proud cheekbones and large, pleading, sunken eyes.

Anton's nose pricked at the memory of the caustic disinfectant which had struggled to eradicate the smell of sickness and shit. He remembered bathing the bedsores and spooning soup into his husband's mouth even as he threw it back up in stringy strands which dribbled down his chin. And all the time those eyes were watching him as he forced another spoonful past his teeth; watching as he caught up the vomit and folded it back past his pale, thin lips. Those round, dark eyes, frightened and accusing at the same time.

He knew. In the end Matteo knew.

Long after he might have had the strength to push away the spoon or topple the bowl from his hands, Matteo knew that he was being slowly poisoned.

A rumbling bellow tore through the tunnels. Anton whipped his head towards the dark entrance to the charnel house, but Angelo didn't react. He continued tending to his bones, removing dead flowers and rearranging a wooden rosary, then he raised the envelope, but before he could open it Anton snatched it from his hand.

"Don't say it," Anton said, his voice magnified in this tight underground space. "Don't say his name out loud." He held the envelope over a candle until the flames caught hold. The sharp smell of smoke filled the place while Angelo gawped at him as if he had gone mad.

Another roar rolled towards them through the maze of passageways. It was closer now, and again Angelo didn't seem to hear it. The skulls piled all around watched in silence, and in the flickering gloom Anton now saw Matteo's hollow stare in them, multiplied, lidless and fixed. He could hear the charge of thundering hooved footsteps… and was that the sound of wide horns gouging furrows into the stone walls? It was coming for him, his grief… except he couldn't pretend anymore. That metastasizing creature which had been stabbing and stinging him, trying to envelop him, was not his grief, it was his guilt.

He dropped the curling remains of the card as the flames reached his fingers, then he grabbed the torch Angelo had left on a shelf. He ran without thinking, his only instinct to escape the approaching beast. Angelo called to him, but he could barely hear the words over the grunts and snorts which seemed to charge at him from all around.

The light from his torch bounced across stony walls and arched ceilings as he ducked left and right down tunnels like a rabbit, paying no heed to where he was going. These passageways and chambers felt hotter now. He was out of shape and was soon breathing hard.

The pursuing sounds morphed into something large and chitinous; a scuttling up the walls and across the ceiling which spoke of legs designed to pierce and hold. And he was sure that he could hear the drums and whistles of the carnival parade in the distance. If he could somehow find his way back to that boisterous world above then he would be safe.

He flew around a corner and skinned his knee on a ragged piece of jutting rock. He fell with a grunt and his torch went sprawling. It spun a couple of times, sending crazy shadows whirling around him before it stuttered and went out. He sucked air in through his teeth and clamped a hand to his throbbing knee. His trousers were torn and the skin beneath was sticky and shredded. Something large scuttled past him in the darkness, he felt the breeze as it passed inches from him and he held his breath until the clicking sounds of those many legs were a distant echo.

He tried to steady his breathing. He could feel his heart in his throat and he was wet with sweat. It felt like a sauna down here now. He pushed himself up and his knee throbbed in complaint. He tried to put his weight on it and found that he could only hobble – a kind of shuffling, lopsided gait which wasn't helped by the need to keep his arms held out against the thick darkness.

He lurched in this fashion until he found a rough wall which he followed as best he could, his palm out flat across the pitted stone as if it were ancient braille. He made slow, painful progress in the dark and began to imagine that the walls were embedded with more skulls, and that his fingers were slipping across teeth, worn brows and pointed chins. He recalled cradling Matteo's emaciated head night after night.

Finally, alone with the truth in this absolute blackness, he could drop his mask. The mask of a caring husband and grieving spouse. A little giggle escaped like a rising bubble. He clapped a hand to his mouth but tittering laughter leaked from between his fingers. He felt his mouth spread wide in a distended grin worthy of one of those carnival masks and that made him laugh some more.

He recalled the sickening thrill of holding the small vial over Matteo's espresso for the first time, and the tightness in his throat before he tipped some of the clear liquid into the drink. Then his shrieking fear at his husband's violent and almost immediate reaction; the cramps and vomiting; the ambulance; the certainty that he would be discovered. But then what followed, after Matteo been discharged, the perfect peace of the two of them alone together. Matteo had needed him again.

His distended grin twisted downwards and the laughter which shook him turned easily to sobs. He was alone. Matteo was not down here; he never had been. From somewhere nearby he heard the beast lowing. It sounded as if it was in pain.

He stumbled on blindly, hoping to find a path which would begin to rise, or a set of steps which might lead him back to the surface. In the absence of light the chambers and tunnels he negotiated took on wild and improbable shapes in his mind's eye; paths curved at strange angles and he strayed into rooms that felt so vast he thought he could see faint, distant stars overhead.

The Minotaur gave the labyrinth its meaning. What had it become after Theseus had worked his heroic blade?

There were moments when he thought that he could feel the walls warping and the pathways coalescing around him in new patterns until it felt as if every direction only led him further into a tightening spiral towards the centre.

When he first saw the distant warmth of orange light he thought he must have reached some vast reservoir of magma beneath the volcano, but as he hobbled nearer he saw iron braziers on the narrow walls filled with glowing coals.

He emerged from a small tunnel into a round domed room where a group in red robes and masks stood silent, waiting around a stone altar at the centre. They turned as he approached and he saw that their masks were all skulls, dull and weathered, although his head span with fatigue and heat and he couldn't be sure that these were masks at all.

Without sound the loose ring of figures opened out and he saw an ungainly, ill-defined shape on the altar. In the dim light he could see matted fur, a hoof, and perhaps a kind of tail. Some of the attendants moved to this shape; they lifted it off the altar and held it open between them like heavy laundry. The skin sagged, cloven feet gathered on the stony floor, and the huge, horned head drooped pathetically. Anton advanced, and even though his knee still needled with pain he felt strangely lighter with each step, as if a weight were being removed from around his neck.

The leathery hide hung open at the back, and he stepped in, thrusting his arms in gratefully as his attendants pulled it closed around him. His breath felt hot and sounded loud inside the great head.

They stitched him in, long needles and rough thread doing their quick work. He flexed his hands and stretched his legs inside his musty, itchy new body, and when the job was done the supporting hands let go and his seamsters withdrew into the shadows and away.

He struggled to keep upright under the weight of the giant horns, and when he moaned it sounded like the cattle low of an animal.

He was sure that he could hear the noises of the carnival nearby. They cheered his first, faltering steps. Through ragged eyeholes he saw the tunnels and chambers around him with a new understanding. He bellowed long and loud and with a trudging, stumbling deliberation he tried to find the path which would lead him back to the place he'd been before.

OCTOPUS

The screams that I could hear from my bedroom window came from The Octopus, over the distant pounding of speaker systems and the machinery of fairground rides. The fair had come to town and I was grounded.

Each year towards the end of September the fair arrived, and The Octopus always made everyone scream. It sat squat, more like a robotic spider than an octopus, and its eight crane-like arms spun around that huge, green grinning head. At the end of each rising and falling arm was a little seat where you could cram in with your folks, your friends, or your date (if you were lucky). And as that seat was lifted and spun it turned on its own axis and thrust you against the sides and rattled the screams out of you whilst the multi-coloured bulbs blinked on and off, and the music thudded, thudded, thudded.

Leaning out of my bedroom window to smoke I could just about see the distant attractions over the tops of our neighbor's spindly trees. My breath made clouds in the chill night air and my arms turned to gooseflesh. I could hear the bass notes from the perpetual music like mechanical heartbeats, and the smell of cotton candy, popcorn, and candy apples reached me on the breeze (or so it seemed). And the screams, of course.

The rest of my family were at the fair that night and I was alone in the house. Thirteen going on thirty (or so my mom said). Daddy's Little Girl being punished because of her smart mouth. I sullenly wondered if any of the screams I could hear were theirs. I closed the window to block out the sounds, but past my pale reflection I could still see the whirling rainbows of splintered lights through the trees, as if a UFO had landed a couple of fields over and everybody had gone to see except for me.

I became acutely aware of the house around me, empty and silent. There was going to be a marathon of *The Twilight Zone* on the television, but I wondered if watching that alone would be a bad idea. Of course, I could sneak out. Everyone in town would be at the fair – there was nothing else to do round here – but maybe I could skirt around the edges and try one or two of the stalls without being busted. All my friends would be there. Surely I could keep out of sight of my parents. My younger brothers might be a problem though; if they saw me they'd squeal for sure, but if I ran straight home across the fields I could be home before them. I was gathering up my overcoat, hat, scarf and gloves when there was a knock at the front door.

Years later, in 1986, I moved to New York. I got a job working as a secretary in one of the skyscrapers I'd only ever seen on the television. The place looked like a city from the future when I first arrived. Back home the stars took over after dark, but the lights and buildings of New York City all but obliterated the night sky.

I was on my lunch break one afternoon and found myself in Barnes & Noble, flicking through a hardback book of 19th Century Japanese erotic art. The pages fell open upon a reproduction of a woodblock print called *The Dream of the Fisherman's Wife*. A naked Japanese woman, a shell diver, lay on her back. Her eyes were closed and her head was thrown back, deep in passion. There was a large, salmon-coloured octopus between her legs. Its round eyes bulged and its beak was over her vagina as its tentacles wrapped around her belly and up her arms. She was gripping two of its thick tentacles and pushing down on that alien mouth, whilst a second, smaller octopus gripped her throat, slipped a thin tentacle into her own mouth, and teased her left nipple.

I began to hyperventilate right there on the shop floor. I dropped the book and slowly crumpled to the ground myself. The edges of my vision became blotchy. My heart was beating so fast that I thought I was dying. I couldn't speak; I could barely breathe. I was covered in a sudden, cold sweat, and I was convinced that my heart would stop at any moment as a crowd of people gathered around me, slowly pressing in.

"Give her some room! Let her have some air!" someone was shouting, but it sounded muffled, as if underwater. Someone was tugging at the collar of my blouse and the flashing lights and the pounding bass notes which could travel for miles were all around (although that could have been my heart pounding). The dark spots in my vision hung, thicker and thicker, like squirted blotches of ink, until I fainted.

After that incident I struggled to leave my apartment for a short while. I took some time off work. Janice from the secretarial pool visited a couple of times. She knocked and called out my name, but I never opened the door to her. I checked the lock constantly, sometimes even in the middle of the night if I woke up suddenly. I would push coats up to the bottom of the door like draft excluders.

Did you know that an octopus' body can contort and stretch so that even the larger species can pass through an opening of one inch in diameter?

I tried some meditation and self-hypnosis from a self-help book I'd bought. That stuff was all the rage at the time, the bookstores were full of them. I found myself thinking about the old town fair quite a bit. I hadn't thought about it for years.

I went back to work. Too soon, probably, but we didn't know as much about anxiety and mental health then as we do today. I had to knuckle down, not be so emotional. My boss said as much when I returned to the office: "The team is only as strong as its weakest player, and you want to be a team player don't you?"

At the end of that year, at the office Christmas party, my boss cornered me, stinking of Scotch whisky. He congratulated me on pulling myself together. He was proud of me and wanted to do something to thank me, personally, for all my hard work (beyond the meager bonus we'd seen in our payslips). He made a pass at me while The Ronettes sang "Frosty the Snowman," but thankfully I managed to disentangle myself quite quickly without making him angry.

Back at my apartment that same night, still bundled up in my coat and scarf against a bitter New York winter, I suddenly recalled the time my family had left me alone, grounded, while they went to the fair. I remembered descending the stairs to sneak out when someone began knocking on the front door.

And the knocking didn't stop.

It wasn't angry or insistent, just steady (polite even). It was almost mechanical.

The lights were off downstairs, so I could creep down and through the hall without being spied through the frosted glass either side of the thick wooden door. I slunk into the TV room to the right, and from the window seat in the big bay window I could pull back the lace curtain and see who it was at the door.

A tall, thin man was standing on the stoop under the hazy porch light. He was wearing a black suit and had on a black hat like you see in those old FBI dramas that sometimes get re-run. He really was awfully thin. His arms dangled down at his sides like string on a balloon, and his legs seemed to dangle from his body in the same way, just long enough for his feet to reach the ground. He raised one of those spaghetti arms again and began another round of knocking.

"Hello," he called out. He spoke in a reedy voice and I was surprised the breeze didn't whip it right out of his mouth. "I'm looking for Mr Kane."

I backed away from the window as carefully as I could while he continued to knock. I made my way quietly to the darkened kitchen at the rear of the house, and as soon as I set foot there the telephone on the wall started to ring. I snatched it off the cradle without thinking – how could I pretend there was no one home now? I hoped it was my dad so that I could plead for him to come home immediately, but instead I heard that thin voice coming from the handset.

"I'm looking for Mr Kane," it said calmly, almost plaintive.

Now, you need to remember that there weren't any mobile phones back then. It simply wasn't possible for the man standing on our porch, knocking on our front door, to also be calling on the telephone.

I heard the clattering fairground rides, sounding close enough to set the windows and the crockery on the sideboard rattling, and the screams on the wind, and now there was a kaleidoscope of lights from outside playing across the plain kitchen walls and ceiling.

I held the phone up to my mouth and tentatively spoke.

"There's no Mr Kane here; you've got the wrong house."

The lights and the mechanical clack of the rides and the knocking stopped dead.

I stood in the dark kitchen for a long time, looking down the hall at the silent, black rectangle of the front door. I was certain that this strange, thin man was still on the far side, waiting.

When my family returned that's where they found me, huddled on the kitchen floor clasping the telephone receiver.

On 10 September 1993 I was woken by my phone.

I grabbed it blearily in the dark. The artificial green light from the screen made my hand look strange. I mumbled into it and there were a few moments of silence. I still wasn't properly awake, and then a quiet, colorless voice spoke.

"The octopus is desire. The octopus is death."

Then the call ended.

I stared at the screen, rubbing my eyes, befuddled: an unknown number.

I jumped when the phone rang in my hand again. It was my mom. I answered, and again there were a few moments of silence. I felt my gorge rising. When she did speak it was to tell me that my dad had passed away.

I got the earliest flight home that I could and Jeff, my youngest brother, picked me up from the airport. We talked on the ride back, but fell into silence when we reached the long, rutted track which led up to the farmhouse. It looked just as I'd remembered it; a little smaller, perhaps, a little more run down. But it also looked as if it had just landed in the middle of that plot of land, so strange and so familiar at the same time.

The house was full of people who'd come to pay their respects. I'd spent so long in New York, where you kept to yourself, that I was surprised to see the place so full. My other brother, Rob, was out in the stables doing the chores which waited for no one, and my mom was busy in the kitchen making sure that none of the guests went hungry. Dad was at the funeral home, which was a relief, because I'd dreaded the thought of confronting him lying in state in the TV room.

The day was busy and confusing, and there had been no real time to speak intimately with my mother or brothers about details and arrangements. It was dark by the time the last guests left, and the house was suddenly quiet and felt empty. Mom set about clearing up, but Jeff, Rob and I managed to persuade her that she could leave everything for the night, and that we would do the dishes and clear all the plates and cups away first thing in the morning.

I stepped outside to smoke a cigarette, but found the wide, bright night sky quite overwhelming. It was so vast and silent. Instead I climbed up to my old room and leaned out of the window to smoke, just as I had done as a teenager. I looked out across the empty fields and stubbed my cigarette out on the window frame and threw the butt out onto the tiles. It only occurred to me at that moment that Dad must have known I'd smoked every time he climbed the ladder to clean out the gutters. That brought the first pang of grief I'd felt since my mother's phone call.

That night I lay in my bed, unable to sleep. The silence was palpable.

Ironically, it seemed that I needed the noises of The City That Never Sleeps to help me drift off. That was part of it, of course, but I was waiting as well.

Midnight passed. Then one. Two.

Long after the sounds of the others shuffling around and settling down had ceased, the tentacles squeezed their way through the gaps under the doors downstairs and up through the ground floor floorboards.

Slick and silent, they moved across the hallway and rubbed against the table legs in the kitchen like cats. Questing and eager, they unfurled up the stairs; probing; tasting. And then they were under my bedroom door, tumbling towards me like eager tongues. They coiled up the bedposts and found my feet; my shins; my belly. They rolled over me and wrapped around my arms and thighs; slick; urgent.

My breasts; my throat.
In absolute silence.
All of me.
It was bliss.

NOCTURIA

Deep down Gary knew he was fucking up even as he waded, naked, into the warm ocean water with this strange woman. He was cheating on his girlfriend on the first night of their holiday, a holiday they'd spent the last couple of years saving for.

Spumy waves hit his shins and the shock threatened to douse his anger, an anger which had lent the evening its momentum and allowed him to consider himself the victim in all this. Better to stoke it, that made this drunken act of revenge feel righteous.

This is what you get, he thought. *This is what you get for ruining our holiday.*

Kelly, his girlfriend, had come on her period on the first night of their holiday. The first fucking night! She'd slunk back to the hotel because her cramps were so bad. Well fuck that! He was on holiday; he was going to stay out and have a fucking good time. And each shot at every bar along the strip had been a jab at her: *How do you like this? Or this?* And somewhere along the stumbling, slurring way this horny tart had attached herself to him. She'd slid an arm through his and hadn't let go, despite the cheap engagement ring on her finger. What was her name? Alyssa? Allegra? She'd told him but he couldn't remember.

After the fifth or sixth bar she had taken his arm and led him down to the beach, then her hands were under his shirt and they were kissing. She'd unbuttoned his trousers while his hands were clumsy at her zip, but she helped him shed her clothes. His cock was throbbing like it hadn't done in years and he stoked those coals: to hell with Kelly and her cramps and tears.

"Why can't we do it on the beach?" he said as she walked him into the sea.

"Maybe I'm a mermaid," she replied with a wide smile.

Last chance to back out. The moonlight made dark circles of her small, hard nipples. His erection pointed the way and he followed. She laughed lightly and waded backwards, pulling him deeper, until the Balearic Sea was lapping at their stomachs. What *was* her name? Aliana? Alayna?

The gentle push of the incoming tide made him sway on unsteady legs. He staggered and the sand shifted beneath his feet. She glided towards him, wrapped her arms around his shoulders and they were kissing again. The sound of the sea filled his ears as her salty tongue pushed past his teeth. He squeezed her breasts roughly and she didn't seem to mind, so he sought out one of her nipples and pinched it hard. She made a husky noise of encouragement. His cock was throbbing so much it almost hurt.

She lifted one leg up to his hip and it seemed to coil around him. Then she was up and on him, and he gasped as she pulled his penis inside her. He grabbed hold of her bottom and her breasts were in his face as she began to pump once, twice — was this really fucking happening? — and he couldn't last beyond the third pump. He came and let out a pathetic grunt.

She slid off him and pushed herself away, buoyed by a gentle wave. He began to mumble an apology for coming so soon, but she was hardly paying him any attention.

"Shall we go back in now?" he said, and she shook her head vigorously, sending out droplets that looked like diamonds in the moonlight.

"I want to swim," she said and held out a hand while she kicked away from him, giggling.

Fuck that, he'd seen Jaws. With his erection softening by the second he suddenly sobered up and realised that he was standing waist deep in the sea in a foreign country with his clothes and wallet about to get swallowed by the incoming tide. He'd just fucked a stranger whilst his girlfriend was back at the hotel because he'd acted like a dick. He had truly fucked up. And now this girl was backstroking further out. Was she mental? Sharks fed at night; he'd heard that somewhere. She had matched him drink for drink too; not a great state to go swimming in. If she got into trouble now, or if something started nibbling at her, there was no way he would swim out to help. He began wading back towards the beach and called for her to come in. By the time he reached their two piles of clothes she seemed like a pale spot upon the dark swell.

"Come back in," he called, then muttered, "you crazy bitch" under his breath. She ducked her head underwater as he pulled his trousers on. The most eager waves were almost at his feet now. She popped back up with a splash and the black sea rolled around her. "I'm fucking off now, yeah?" he said.

He watched her, impotent, for another fifteen or so seconds before stomping back up the fine sand. She looked as if she was enjoying herself. She was a big girl. She didn't need him to tell her what to do.

Back at his room he opened the door as quietly as possible and undressed in the dark. He slid into bed next to Kelly, who remained a silent, still bundle. He couldn't tell if she was sleeping or ignoring him. The room began to spin and he almost laughed; that hadn't happened since his teens when he used to drink White Lightning from the bottle with his mates in a field. He closed his eyes and everything rocked as if their mattress was afloat on the sea.

Kelly's breathing was shallow which meant she was awake. He rolled away from her; no point trying to apologise now, what's done was done. What she didn't know wouldn't hurt her. He had taken things too far, though, but he had the rest of the holiday to make it up to her. He would take her out for a nice meal or something. Despite the rolling of the bed and the spinning room Gary soon fell asleep.

Hours later he roused from dreams of running water. It was still dark and his bladder throbbed with an urgency which had woken him. He had another erection but this one was borne from a desperate need to urinate. Kelly was breathing deeply now and he eased himself out of the bed. Movement made the pressure worse; he felt as if he was going to burst.

He kept the bathroom light off because he didn't want to wake Kelly. The porcelain of the toilet bowl glowed dully like a skull. He lifted the lid and sat down; he didn't want to risk his aim in the dark after so many drinks. He pushed but nothing happened. The discomfort of feeling so full intensified but nothing came out.

He paused and took some deep breaths.

Relax and let it flow, he thought, and wondered if he should turn on a tap to get things moving. His bare feet felt gritty on the bathroom tiles; he still had sand from the beach stuck to his soles. *Fucking hell, what a night. What a mad, mad night.* He thought of Alana or Alyssa; the salt water on her skin; the feel of her breasts under his grasping hands – he suddenly let go of a hot, steady flow of urine. The needling sting which came with it made him suck air in through his teeth. The sharp smell of piss filled the small room and it felt as if someone had slid a thin, red-hot wire up his urethra. He tried to stop the flow but it wouldn't be dammed; on it gushed, and all the time the tip of his cock felt like it was being stung by wasps. He clenched his jaw to keep from crying out. Tears sprang to his eyes and he had to hold on until he'd emptied his bladder.

When he had finished he scrambled for the cord to the small light above the sink. He pulled the wrong one at first and turned on a noisy extractor fan before finding the one he wanted. He blinked against the harsh white light, cheeks stained with tears, and examined the fiery tip of his penis. It was red, a little inflamed, but with the pain he'd felt he was sure that it would look much worse than it did.

So much for shagging in the sea, he thought.

He turned on the tap and splashed cold water onto the angry little hole. He wondered if Kelly might have some cream for it, but how could he explain why he needed it? He turned out the light and made his way gingerly back to bed. He lay awake for a long time before finally falling back to sleep.

*

When he woke it was light and Kelly had gone.

He looked for his phone, worried that he'd lost it on the beach, but it was in his trouser pocket on the floor where he'd left his clothes the night before. It was 11.37am. No messages or missed calls from her. She'd probably gone down to get the all-inclusive breakfast. His stomach made its presence felt; he was famished. He could also feel the beginnings of a hangover and his mouth tasted foul.

He brushed his teeth under the hot spray of the shower, hoping to blast his impending headache away. He began absentmindedly scratching his genitals, and as soon as he became conscious of the itching it worsened.

That bitch better not have given me crabs last night, he thought.

He got out and towelled himself down, rubbing vigorously between his legs. That just made the itch worse. He searched through Kelly's lotions and potions and found a bottle of After Sun for sunburn; that had to be kind to skin, right? He squeezed out a palmful and felt instant relief from the cool gel.

Thank fuck for that, he thought. His stomach complained again. *Right, time for some grub.*

He spotted Kelly as he entered the restaurant; she was at a far table and was talking to a member of staff, a man. He wanted to go straight over to them but he was ravenous now. It was a buffet set up so he grabbed a tray and a plate and joined the slow-moving queue, checking on his girlfriend and that talkative waiter the whole time. *Shouldn't he be doing his job and not chatting up the guests?* He piled his plate high, already planning a return trip, and strode towards them with a bellicose grin on his face.

"Morning," he said, and chose a seat which forced the bloke to step to one side. "What are we talking about?" Kelly scowled at him, then turned to smile at the young lad.

"Thank you, Ignacio," she said, "you've been very helpful." Ignacio, or whatever his name was, left quickly while Gary shovelled food into his mouth, his eyes on Kelly the whole time.

"He was telling me about places to visit in the Old Town," she said. "I thought it might be nice to see some of the island away from the beaches and bars." He ate some more then laid his fork down with a sigh.

"How are you feeling today?" he asked.

"Like you care?"

"Look, I'm sorry, alright?"

"You were really cruel last night."

"I know. I'm sorry, babes," he said. "I was drunk. We'd both been looking forward to this holiday for so long; both grafting to put money aside. I wanted it to be perfect and I've mucked it up." Kelly was moving the remains of her breakfast around her plate with a fork.

"I was looking forward to it as well, you know?" she said.

"I know, baby. Let me make it up to you, yeah? What sort of places did old Inglese back there recommend?"

"Ignacio," she said with a smile. A small one, but a smile, nonetheless. He was off the hook.

He listened with one ear while she talked about tours of the Old Town; churches; markets. They put on a good spread here, but the toast, slightly congealed beans, bacon, and rheumy scrambled eggs weren't touching the sides. He nodded along and gulped at a mug of coffee until Kelly had finished. He was desperate to get back to the buffet for a second helping.

"Sounds great, love. We can do all that for sure." He took another gulp of coffee. "Another day, though, yeah? I'm hanging after last night; my punishment for being a knob. I could really do with a day on the beach today, how does that sound?"

Kelly nodded quietly.

"You're the best," he said. "Love you, babes."

He was up and away to the buffet queue before she could reply.

*

The beach was packed. They claimed a spot with their towels then slathered themselves with coconut smelling sun cream. She read a trashy paperback in the shade of her wide, floppy straw hat, and he tried to make himself comfortable, hoping his hangover would pass soon. There were a couple of French girls sunbathing topless nearby, but he mostly kept his gaze off them. There was no point in winding Kelly up again.

The sun and the sound of the surf soon made him drowsy. He wondered idly whether the woman from last night was somewhere on this beach. What a fucking disaster that would be. Maybe she really had drowned. Maybe her torso would wash up onto the sand like that swimmer in Jaws, in front of all these families.

As he thought of her he began scratching his groin again. The itch became more insistent but he couldn't do anything about it without looking as if he were fondling himself. The prickling spread.

"Think I'll take a little dip and cool off," he said and got up.

He weaved a path through fellow sunbathers, towels, and loungers, and made as straight a path as he could towards the sea. The whole way there he had to fight to keep his hands off his crotch. It felt as if someone was brushing nettles across his junk. Had that slag really given him a dose of something? That would be the rest of the holiday fucked if she had. Even if Kelly were up for it in a day or two he couldn't pass it on to her, could he? That would be as good as a signed confession. He wondered if his travel insurance would cover it, and whether Kelly would find out if he tried to make a claim. He wasn't enamoured with the idea of seeing a Spanish doctor anyway. Better to wait and see his own GP back home, so long as he could keep from scratching himself to shreds till then.

He strode into the water and his hand was down his Bermuda shorts the moment the first wave surged forwards to meet him, but as soon as his bottom half was submerged the itching subsided. He let out a groan of relief as the chilly water did its job.

Back up to my balls in the sea again, he thought with a dry chuckle.

The rest of the morning went by lazily, and after a bite for lunch they returned to the beach to see out the day. That evening they washed, got dressed up, and went out for the meal he'd promised her. All evening he drank nothing but soft drinks to appease her. That night as he fell asleep he congratulated himself for smoothing everything over so nicely.

He woke again in the middle of the night with the pressing, urgent need to pee. Kelly had long since rolled over to her side of the bed and he stood up tentatively and made the trip to the bathroom in darkness again. He must have overdone it with the Cokes at dinner. He padded onto the cold tiles of the bathroom floor, much more clear-headed than the night before, and aimed into the dark shadow of the toilet bowl. As soon as he started to pee he felt the same sear of hot pain shoot right up inside him. He doubled over, splashing the toilet seat, the floor, and his own legs and feet. The burning sting shot up his urethra over and over, like a sewing machine needle, and this time he did cry out in pain.

"You alright?" Kelly called groggily.

In the bathroom he bit into his hand to keep from crying out again. His urine was coming in fitful spurts, and each time it was accompanied by another electric shock of pain. He could hear Kelly rousing and he hadn't locked or even properly closed the bathroom door.

"I'm fine," he managed to say between painful squirts. "Just tripped and stubbed my toe in the dark. I'll be back to bed in a mo."

A dull throb remained once his bladder had emptied itself. It hurt, but it was infinitely preferable to the feeling of pissing out pins. He gently pushed the bathroom door closed, quietly locked it, then turned on the light. He held his aching cock gingerly, but beyond a little redness he saw no damage. He'd pissed everywhere, though. It was all over the floor and he could feel it down his legs. He'd have to clean it up once the ache had died down a little.

He gathered up fistfuls of toilet paper and began mopping up his mess. His urine looked dark, like cheap cider, even though he'd kept well hydrated all day. He wondered if he had kidney stones, that was supposed to be as painful as giving birth for a bloke, wasn't it?

The pain between his legs slowly subsided like the receding tide. He washed his feet and legs from the sink – the shower would wake Kelly and prompt questions – and once he'd dried up and flushed the toilet he went back to bed and lay waiting for sleep to claim him. It took a long time.

*

The next morning he was ravenously hungry again. Kelly sent him down to the restaurant so she could pack for their trip to the Old Town in peace.

"Bloody hell, we're only going on a day trip," he said when she joined him with a bulging bag slung over her shoulder. She ate a light breakfast while he nipped to the small shop which adjoined the hotel. He bought a large bottle of water, telling Kelly that he needed to stay hydrated, but in truth he wanted to flush out this bloody urinary tract infection as quickly as possible.

Their taxi rattled through arid countryside and dropped them outside the Old Town by the island's main harbour. Sea and sky sat like bright swatches of blue, one laid on top of the other, and whitewashed buildings crowded the foot of the hill which rose above the harbour.

Beyond the ancient stone walls of the town lay a mess of branching, crisscrossing cobbled lanes which ascended to the medieval fort at the summit. A sunny labyrinth of brief tunnels, alcoves, squares, and balconies carved into the slopes. This wasn't what Gary had come to the island for. He'd imagined them sampling the nightlife; getting hammered; maybe even scoring some drugs and clubbing till sunrise like he had in his twenties. He wasn't into all this culture but figured if he traipsed around the places Kelly wanted to see for one day then he'd be able to set the agenda for the rest of the holiday. So, he followed her up the narrow, cobbled streets and kept his tongue in his mouth each time she stopped to read yet another plaque or take a picture of a doorway or an arch.

Around noon they visited the Museum of Archaeology and joined a slow snake of tourists filing past exhibits in glass cases. They all seemed to him to be full of broken pots, time-worn busts and crusty jewellery. Many of them depicted women and fish, which he imagined were the sole preoccupations of a bygone island community. "Fucking and fishing," as he put it. By now the litre of water he'd drunk was beginning to make itself known.

"Need a piss," he stage-whispered to Kelly and peeled away from yet another pot, this one depicting a woman's face with wavy hair like a crown of eels. He found the gents and locked himself in a cubicle, then sat with his hands on his knees, braced against the anticipated pain. He released a trickle at first, expecting the harsh sting, but none came. The tension across his shoulders vanished and he let it flow. He let out a contented moan and revelled in the sound of urine hitting toilet water.

Back in the museum he looked for Kelly amongst the shuffling crowd but couldn't see her. He moved through the rooms but she wasn't there, so he made his way outside. The sun hit him, then the realisation that Kelly wasn't waiting for him out there. He looked up and down the narrow sloping street. Tourists passed like listless clouds but she wasn't among them. He spotted a couple of craft shops further up the hill and jogged up to them. She was in neither. He checked his phone: no calls, no messages. He called her, but he went straight to her voicemail.

"I've lost you, babes," he said after the recorded message. "I'm waiting outside the museum; come find me and I'll treat you to some lunch."

He walked back down to the museum, scanning the crowd, expecting to see her waiting outside and wondering how they'd missed one another, but she wasn't there. He called her again and went straight to voicemail a second time. He floundered, then jogged a little way down the hill to where the street split into two. One path continued its cobbled descent, and the other angled off into a steep set of steps which climbed again in another direction.

As he stood there and span like a lighthouse, scouring the tanned and burnt faces, did he catch a familiar face climbing those steep steps? Not Kelly, but was that the girl from the beach, turning away from him, smiling to herself? For a strange moment he pictured Kelly with that woman, their heads together, whispering and laughing.

He checked his phone again. Nothing.

"Come on, come on," he muttered to himself. "Where the fuck are you?" He called her again. Voicemail.

There was nothing else he could do but climb back to the museum. At the ticket desk he showed them a picture of her on his phone and asked if they had seen her, but they couldn't understand him (or pretended not to, he suspected). With his frustration growing and anger not far behind he began to shout "Police! Police!" and they understood that all right.

The police arrived twenty minutes later. No doubt they'd been told a drunken English tourist was causing trouble and it took him a while to explain in stilted English – peppered with childlike Spanish – that his girlfriend had gone missing.

"You had fight?" one officer asked in a thick accent which rankled him.

"A couple of nights ago, yeah, but it's all sweet now."

"You fought? She left?"

"No, mate, she didn't leave, she's missing. I went to the toilet," he googled the word on his phone, "inodoro... I went inodoro, yeah? And when I came out she was gone. Missing." He googled again. "Bloody hell, des... despa..."

"Desaparegut?" the officer said, then blew on his fingers and opened them up, miming a puff of smoke.

"Yes," Gary said. "Yes. Si."

The officer nodded slowly then turned to his colleagues. They spent a long time talking in Spanish or Catalan, which wound Gary up even further. The next two hours tested his patience to the limit. He left with the police who drove him to the station. They took his statement and kept asking about the argument, which just wound him up. They asked him for a picture of Kelly. They made calls to his hotel. He was left sitting on his own for long stretches of time and was just about to start kicking up a fuss when a policeman he'd not seen till now approached. He was overweight with sun-creased skin across his forehead and at the corners of his eyes. His thick black moustache had a sprinkle of grey in it.

"We have been to your hotel," he said after he introduced himself. "They have a key; we looked in your room. Some disturbance there."

"What do you mean disturbance?"

The policeman pulled a face as if he'd smelt something unpleasant, then said, "Empty drawers. Lots of men's clothes, only a few for the lady. One passport."

"What do you mean?"

"Then we called the airport."

"I don't understand what you're telling me."

"Your lady has left, sir."

"What?"

"She has left the island." He turned his hand into a plane taking off.

"No, no, that's bullshit." Red-faced, Gary stood. He was about to do something stupid when his phone pinged. He felt the colour of his neck and face darken as he read the message. He thought of the bulging bag Kelly had brought down from their hotel room that morning.

"Is that the señorita?" the policeman asked.

At that moment Gary felt a wet warmth spread across his crotch. The policeman made a little noise and stepped back.

"Are you alright?" he asked with genuine concern in his voice. Gary wanted to explain about his infection, all the water he'd been drinking. His rage deflated into embarrassment and he wanted to be gone from here. He looked down at the small patch which had soaked through his trousers. He hadn't wet himself. It was blood.

*

Kelly knew she shouldn't use her phone on the plane but she didn't want to wait until she got back to the UK to message Gary, that would be cruel. It could do no harm to let him know now; she was the air, she was leaving him, he couldn't stop her.

She'd known it was over between them some months ago but had hoped things would improve. She had convinced herself that this holiday could be a chance to mend things between them. What an idiot.

On that first night, watching him getting drunk, she knew she wouldn't be able to bear his touch so she pretended that she was on her period. She made up her mind to leave him right then, not because of his sudden temper, but the numb realisation that he was incapable of noticing that she'd missed her last three periods.

On the lonely walk back to the hotel that numbness began to wear off and the dam she'd shored up against her growing sadness finally cracked. At the dark water's edge, feet in the surf, she'd pulled her engagement ring off and flung it into the sea.

"You can have him," she shouted at the dark waves.

She had called her mum in tears when she got back to the room. It was the first time they'd spoken properly in over a year. Her mother had been resolute: "You're coming home. Your dad and I will buy your ticket, I'll message you the flight details. We can pick you up at the airport and go and collect your things before he's even back in the country."

The next morning a nice young waiter had told her the best way to get to the airport, near the Old Town. She never expected Gary to join her on that trip so she had to pretend everything was fine and find a moment to slip away amongst the crowds.

Now she was strangely calm. She was sitting in a cramped aisle seat, but if she leant forwards she could see the white tops of clouds through the oval window. She laid a hand on her belly. She'd have to tell her parents about this as well. She didn't want to keep it.

She idly rubbed at her ring finger where her engagement ring had been not two days ago. There wasn't even a tan line. He hadn't even noticed that she wasn't wearing it.

*

During the taxi ride back to the north of the island Gary stewed. He covered the spotty stain on the front of his trousers as best he could and read Kelly's message again:

I'm sorry. I can't do this anymore. Don't try to contact me. I'm changing my number when I get back home.

The hotel room was a silent testament to hurried activity. Drawers and wardrobe doors were open, the contents were disturbed, although he couldn't tell whether the police or Kelly packing in a hurry had left the mess.

He kicked his sandals off and carefully peeled his trousers and underwear away from his body. The dark, bloody stain gave him the weirdest impression that the messy room was a crime scene.

He checked his penis in the bathroom, touching it tentatively. The tip was angry and sore. It looked as if it was gummed up with a brownish, viscous gunk. He washed himself then sat on the edge of the bed to google "blood in urine;" "kidney infection blood in urine;" "STI blood in urine." After half an hour he was none the wiser. He might have anything from a urinary tract infection or a kidney infection to gonorrhoea or even cancer. He dropped his phone onto the bed and looked around at the half-emptied drawers.

Fucking bitch, he thought. Then he said it out loud and started repeating it, not even sure if he meant Kelly, the woman from the other night, or some chimera of the two smeared together. Soon he was shouting it and his anger – so easily tapped these days – spewed out.

He wrecked the room. He kicked the hanging drawers to pieces then yanked the wardrobe door off its hinges. He tore off the bedsheets, put a foot through the thin bathroom door, pulled down the shower rail, and cracked the mirror by throwing a ceramic soap dish at it.

After that explosion he sat for ten minutes in silence at the end of the bed. He expected a knock at the door – hotel security, maybe even the police again – but when no one came he had a shower, extracted some clean clothes from the mess of his room, retrieved his wallet and phone and went to the bar on the ground floor.

*

As Gary drank, gravity continued its implacable work. The sun set and the moon rolled into the sky, dragging the ocean in its net. The tide changed and the waters began to flow inwards once again.

*

The music in the bar was pounding. Some Europop shit that would probably be stuck in his head for days. He sat in the corner, clutching his glass with one hand and scratching his bedevilled groin beneath the table with the other.

Throughout the night his thoughts darkened and curled in on themselves, like the edges of a burning book. They vacillated between Kelly's betrayal and the trampy one-night stand who'd dosed him. He brooded on how he could make Kelly suffer once he got back home and what he might do to that other bitch if he came across her in one of these bars tonight.

The pain was radiating out from his genitals and bladder now, and with it the almost constant urge to pee. He finished his drink and staggered to the toilets at the rear of this place once more. He fumbled with his zip, swaying, and hovered in front of the urinal. His penis was the colour of a bruise and the waves of pain redoubled as he squeezed out a few dribbles of viscous gunk. He dabbed the end with some toilet paper, sniffed, and made his way back to the bar for another drink.

As the night wore on he moved from place to place, but they all had the same lager on tap and they all seemed to be playing that same song. His rage required gasoline so he started ordering tequila shots with his lager.

The next time he visited the bathroom it felt as if he were passing tiny granules of broken glass. He cried out and slid down the side of the cubicle.

"Tha bish," he slurred to himself, crumpled on the stained floor. Then he roared, "Tha fuggn bish!" He pushed himself up and cleaned himself off as best he could. At the sink he splashed cold water onto his face. He blinked slowly at his reflection. He'd given her everything. This was how she repaid him?

The pints were weighing heavy on his bladder so he moved to vodka and coke (plus the tequila shots). The bass speaker of this place seemed to drive the pain in his groin. There was a hen do on the dance floor. He'd gotten lucky his first night here, why not try his luck again now that he was a free man? He swayed over to them, head pounding, music banging. He tried to strike up a conversation until one of them told him to piss off over the music. He hurled a volley of insults at them as he left, calling them dykes and frigid. He wasn't going to spend any more money in this shithole.

On his way off the dancefloor, glass in hand, he felt as if someone had run up and rammed a knife into his balls. He staggered and almost dropped to the floor. He could hear shrieks of laughter behind him as he gasped for breath like a goldfish plucked from its bowl. He felt wetness spread across his crotch again and saw dark spots blooming across his tan trousers. He managed to stand up almost straight and staggered back to the bathroom.

The music was only slightly muted in the toilets. The bass still hammered through everything; it felt as if it was inside his skull. A couple of guys at the urinals turned to look at him as he scrambled into a cubicle. He didn't care what he looked like; it felt as if someone was pulling barbed wire out through his cock.

He placed his half full vodka and coke on the cistern and fumbled at his trousers and briefs. They were soaked with the bloody liquid which was still oozing from him like a squeezed spot. It smelt musky and rancid. His penis was erect, horribly engorged. Most of it was an alarming purplish colour and the tip had ballooned to almost twice its normal size. The foreskin around it was shiny and taut like sausage skin, ready to split.

He tried to pull his foreskin down off the distended, seeping head of his penis, but simply touching it made him gag with pain. His face was covered in snot and tears which he wiped away with a sleeve. The veins up the shaft of his penis stood out darkly and he could see his pulse in them. Every beat of his heart caused a fresh surge of pain which made his head spin and threatened blackout. He'd reached a point of crying which was just inaudible, wheezing exhalations.

He reached for his drink and poured the scant contents over his burning cock, hoping there was enough alcohol there to sterilise it, then he brought the glass down on the cistern tank. With a shaking hand he collected a curved shard of glass and held it against his agonised foreskin. He was hyperventilating as he put the edge of the glass to the stretched, complaining skin there. He had to relieve the pressure before it tore of its own accord. The music was still banging and insistent; it felt as if this was all he had ever known.

He held his breath, tears making his vision swim, and ran the shard down his skin. There was an instant gout of thick, dark blood and then a glut of yellowish pus. This new needle of pain set off all the nerve endings in that part of his body like fire alarms. Unconsciousness came like mercy.

He only blacked out for thirty or forty seconds, though. He came to on the cubicle floor with his trousers around his ankles and his lap covered in blood. His penis was still on fire but the terrible tearing of skin had subsided. He began to moan as he looked at his mangled body. A bloody flap of foreskin jiggled in the air with each deep breath. He needed help. He had to get out of here.

He rose heavily, leaning on the toilet, slipping in the blood which looked to be full of rubbery clots. By the time he had pulled up his trousers his shaking hands were a red mess. He clutched the top of his trousers, holding them loosely, unable to do them up, and left the toilets on unsteady legs.

Back in the club the music boomed, and now the place was full of smoke from a machine by the small DJ booth. Gary pushed his way through the crowd. He had to get outside, no one would be able to hear him in here. To them he just looked like another English tourist who'd had too much to drink. He couldn't remember where he was but hoped that he was near to the hotel. They'd be able to call an ambulance for him from reception. Or he could just scream for help in the street. He found his way to a dingy staircase and climbed back out into the warm night air.

Then he heard the sea.

Urgency receded and his racing thoughts coalesced into the memory of his earlier itching discomfort being washed away in the balmy salt water. His legs were moving before rational thought could take hold, jerky and stiff like a mannequin come to life. He needed the water; somehow he knew that deep inside his guts.

He crossed the road and staggered down the beach. He could see the white foam in lines like brushstrokes on black sea. At the water's edge he let go of his trousers and his strides became even more awkward. Small waves crashed one over another as if rushing to be the one which meet him first. He waded out until the water was at his waist, and his hot agony suddenly numbed to a dull throb. His pain now came to him as if from somewhere far away.

The moon was a thin crescent. It looked like one of the curved swords he'd seen in the museum earlier that day.

Was that today? he thought. It felt like such a long time ago.

Something disturbed the water in front of him. Bubbles. Then her head broke the surface, her hair stuck slick to her neck and bare shoulders. Gary gawped, dumfounded, light-headed with relief.

"Eivissa," he said; her name was on his lips as if her being here was the most natural thing in the world.

She rose further to stand in front of him, naked. Her skin looked iridescent. Her lips were perhaps more pronounced than he remembered, and her eyes were flatter and further apart. He murmured her name again and began to weep. He wanted to tell her everything but his words were coming out in a ceaseless burble. Still, she nodded and glided towards him. She put her arms around him and he fell into her slick embrace. For a moment he felt completely unburdened.

She was close now. He could feel her legs against his. They seemed to coil around his own and hold them fast and apart. He studied her face but could read nothing in the cold, dark discs of her eyes.

The pressure began to build inside him again; urgent, insistent. It radiated out from his bladder and he was overwhelmed with the urge to push, no matter the pain. He couldn't hold it back.

He let it go and screamed as he evacuated a stream of thousands upon thousands of tiny bodies. They were eager to burst free, more of them than his body could stand, and they tore through his genitals, churning the water around him into frothing, popping life. Still they came, needle teeth widening the ragged holes they had already made, spilling out of him. Small, squirming bodies which turned in the cold water and began to swim back towards the hot gush of blood and the warm flesh which had birthed them. So much flesh. Enough for hungry newborn mouths to gorge themselves upon.

ONE HEART

Can a memory be a ghost, even a forgotten memory?

What about a genetic memory?

*

I AM, I AM, I AM.

Those liquid words boomed all around me for as long as I could remember; warm; steady; powerful. For a time that was all there was.

I AM, I AM, I AM.

Then I was given hands with which to touch and reach enough to explore. I struck out in search of that voice and I touched my brother's face. I was no longer alone.

We lay together, clung to one another, and those warm beating words enveloped us. Soon I could hear the faint echo of those words pulsing inside his chest, and for the first time I felt that tiny rhythm inside me also.

I AM, I AM, I AM.

Our world contracted in violent spasms. The words pounded angrily around us as we were squeezed. My brother was pulled from my grasp. I tried to hold onto him, but his foot was slick and I lost my grip.

I was alone and squeezed again, forced out, thrashing in emptiness.

I could no longer hear the voice.

The weak words inside my own chest faltered.

I am, am I.

I cried out. Once.

*

The dream ended suddenly, but Adam was not suddenly awake. He could still feel the edges of sleep and tried to swim back down, but there was a crack in the curtains and a finger of late morning sun poked him, harassing him reluctantly into the real world. He rubbed his gritty eyes and felt Cassy move beside him. He squirmed gracelessly to face her in time to see her nose wrinkle before she pulled the covers up over her head.

"Morning," he said softly. She made a noise of protest. "Typical student," he muttered and stroked her stomach underneath the bedclothes.

"S'alright for you, dropout," she slurred sleepily, "you weren't the one getting kicked all night. Some big dreams you were having; all night muttering and twitching, keeping me awake. At least tell me I've slept through my nine o'clock lecture."

"I don't remember any dreams," he said.

"You are joking."

"What was I saying?"

"Nothing, just nonsense words, now shut up and let me sleep through my lecture."

"It's Saturday," Adam said matter-of-factly to her back as she rolled away from him, dragging most of the covers with her. She harrumphed a non-verbal reply and hunkered down deeper into the covers.

Reaching for the floor on his side of the bed Adam retrieved his cigarettes and the empty beer can he'd been using as an ashtray. The smell of stale beer and cigarette butts stung his nostrils. He smoked a philosophical cigarette in silence and about half an hour later Cassy turned back round, more awake now, and snaked an arm around his waist.

"Saturday?" she said.

"Uh-huh." She kissed his chest and wriggled a little closer, letting her hand glide down to his thigh.

"Have you decided whether you're going to see her?" she asked. Her nails traced the inside of his leg, quickening his pulse.

"I haven't decided."

"Because if you *are* going," a rude smile played across her lips, "I'll have to give you your birthday present now." Her fingers stopped playing and she ducked her head beneath the covers. By now his heart was pounding in earnest.

*

Once a few stations had passed Adam relaxed a little into the swaying rhythm of the train. He laid his head back and gazed out of the smeared window. The nap of the seat cover brushed his cheek as he rocked slightly.

Urban greys rushed past the scratched NO SMOKING sticker on the window, but they soon gave way to terraced back gardens, then splashes and streaks of suburban green.

As the train slowed for each station he became more attentive, mentally ticking each one off a list that brought him closer to his destination. Between stations, though, his mind wandered with the syncopated clacking of the tracks. He closed his eyes against the sun which angled into his carriage, turning it a curious yellow. Behind his eyelids the sunlight became red and veiny, pulsing. In between those flashes his memory grasped at the ragged tatters of his dreams which were still flapping at the back of his mind.

...*Running*...

The sun warmed his face and the train rocked him gently.

...*Running through plush gardens, the sharp smell of grass, dew cooling his feet. Impossible fruits hanging heavy upon trees, their sweet juices spilling down his chin as he bit into their flesh. A strange sun above him sending down warmth and love in hot, regular waves. The long grass tripping him. Soft falling. Rolling through the undergrowth; his heart beating in time with the pulsing heat above. Someone was there with him...*

The train lurched and slowed, breaking his reverie.

Bricks and buildings had built up again outside and the train was coasting now, gliding towards his stop. He pushed himself up from his seat and made his way to the end of the carriage. Once the train had juddered to a standstill he opened the door and hopped down, one of only a few other people who were disembarking. He headed for the bridge that would take him across to the other side of the tracks and out into the afternoon.

Outside the station a woman was selling flowers from a small stall. Adam paused, decided, then strolled towards her. The flower seller looked up from her paper, smiled at him, and tucked it out of sight beneath her seat.

"Yes, love?" she asked, rubbing her hands against a pretend chill.

"Uh," he surveyed the bouquets on offer. "What can I get for a fiver?"

"For a girlfriend?"

"Mother."

"Mothers prefer a mixed bunch. We'll save the dozen roses for the young ladies, eh?" She plucked a colourful spray from her selection. As Adam wrangled the change from a deep coat pocket and began counting it out in his palm she considered him, perhaps felt a little sorry for him, then lifted a second bunch and held it out, saying: "Two for a fiver today. Special offer for good sons".

"I don't know I'm that," he mumbled, accepting the charity, "but thanks."

The walk from the station to his mother was a little like playing hide and seek with déjà vu. It had been just over five years since he'd last been here, and in that time things had changed just enough to keep him uncertain that he was heading in the right direction.

Good son. Those words made him uncomfortable. He'd been thinking of visiting for a while now but in all honesty it had been Cassy who'd given enough gentle encouragement to turn thoughts into action. Once he'd finally opened up to her and shared some of his regrets she'd simply said, "Why not just go?" And he couldn't come up with a good reason not to. Maybe he'd get Cassy some flowers too, on the way back, if the stall was still there. He'd call her from the train; perhaps she could meet him at the station and they could go out for a drink.

The further he walked the more the bustle and traffic was replaced by quieter streets. Houses instead of shops. He could see the steeple between the houses now and he clutched his thinly wrapped flowers a little tighter. At the end of the street he turned left, slipping into the shadow of a grand oak tree, and took the slight incline at a steady pace. The church was emerging now, and a rook cawed somewhere in the grounds.

The Church of the Immaculate Conception. He passed through the gate and the pebbled path that led to the main entrance clicked underfoot. He followed it for a few steps before cutting across the grass and circling round to the rear of the building.

He weaved a path between slanting headstones and made his way towards her. He came up quietly and stood for a few moments, heart in his throat, before softly saying, "Hello, Mum." The rook cawed again, further away now. "I've brought some flowers," he said, feeling a little foolish, but he laid them down all the same, in front of her headstone.

*

I am, I am, I am.

I am a ghost of sorts, existing inside a pre-birth memory that is never called upon. I course through his blood and swell in his chest and thud in his ears, but he cannot hear me.

He has forgotten.

*

Cassy noticed a difference in him almost straight away; nothing dramatic, but she marked it, nonetheless. A few days passed before she could put her finger on what it was, though. They were out for the evening, some small pub on the way to see a movie, and he was saying: "I'm remembering so much more about her since I went to her grave. It's like I'd locked myself out from my own childhood, but it's all coming back now." That was when she realised: *He's not frowning.*

Over the next few months his smile came more easily. She found ways of getting closer to him that he had blocked off before. She eased cautiously into this new stage of their relationship but never spoke about it to him for fear of scaring it away like smoke. He spoke more hopefully about finding a job, talked more openly about everything; they talked more and touched more and shared silences. She felt this new thing that clamoured in her heart to be named, but she ignored it. Best to let it alone, she thought. Best not to lean on it now, while it's still fragile.

*

"How did the interview go?" Cassy asked as he answered the front door.

"Pretty good. You coming up?" Adam jogged up the stairs and she gently closed the door and followed. Music was blaring from his bedsit and he turned it down before she reached his room.

"Cup of tea?" he asked from the other side of the room, reaching for a half-smoked cigarette that balanced on the ashtray. The window was open and he placed himself on the windowsill, leaving the only chair in the room free for her. He was still wearing his shirt and tie from the job interview and she studied him approvingly. The small room smelt faintly of the aftershave he'd used and it seemed to her as if someone else had been here moments before but had left just before she'd arrived.

"Have you been burgled?" she cast her eyes around before tiptoeing towards the chair through the clutter on the floor.

"Just going through some of my Mum's stuff." He held his cigarettes out but she shook her head.

"When will you hear?" she asked.

"Mmm? Oh, they're interviewing all next week as well, so not for a fortnight at least. Trying not to get my hopes up, but at the very least it's good to get some job interview practice. Check this out." He leaned across his bed, plucked something off the duvet and handed it to her. It was a photo album.

"Oh my God!" Cassy squealed, "little baby Adam!" She flipped through the photos, at turns ah-ing then giggling.

"There's one right at the back," he was leaning over her shoulder now. "Must've been taken when I was only a few hours old." She flipped to the last page and indeed there was a picture all on its own of a tiny baby, eyes closed, wrapped in a white blanket.

"Sickly child," she murmured.

"Poor lighting," he defended.

"You're almost blue!" She flipped the photo over. On the back in thin black biro was a date, Adam's birthday, and a quote which she read: "And they shall be one flesh, one heart, one soul – EMMA".

"You ever hear of a poem called 'Emma'?" he asked.

She shook her head. "There's a book by Jane Austen. The quote doesn't ring a bell, though." She flipped the picture back over to consider the tiny, wrinkled grey face.

*

Cassy woke smoothly to the noise but wasn't sure if it had come from inside the room or from her sleep. She could smell smoke and stretched a hand across to the other side of the bed. It was empty. The noise came again and she sat up a little. Adam was in the shadows, sitting on the chair in the far corner, the tip of a cigarette bobbing where his hand shook. He was crying. She slid out of bed and as soon as he realised that she was awake he fell quiet and began to rub at his eyes. She sat by his feet and rested her head in his lap.

"Hey," she whispered.

"Didn't mean to wake you, sorry," he said, his voice a little croaky. He took a pull on his cigarette.

"What's the matter?" she asked.

"Oh…" he was getting control of his voice quickly; the tears had stopped. "Just, sometimes… it's nothing."

"Tell me." She took one of his hands and kissed them. "Tell me."

"It's embarrassing."

"No, it's not. It's just the two of us here." He was quiet for a while, and then she felt him shaking silently in the darkness. He was crying again.

"I just get these thoughts sometimes."

She held him until he stopped crying. Then she took his hand and led him back to the bed. They lay in each other's arms in silence for a long time;

she could feel his heart. Then they moved closer; came together. Arms, lips and legs joined.

Afterwards she held him until he fell asleep, but while they had been connected something had passed between them.

*

Months passed and the dreams still came – creeping up slowly, almost nightly now – to broil and billow in the back of her sleeping mind.

Dreams of Adam in the garden, falling, hugging the earth.

Dreams of Adam at a mirror, pushing through the mercurial surface. At play with his reflection, forming strangely limbed creatures, all fleshy loops and melted forms.

Dreams of Adam gagging, coughing up his heart to steam and throb on the floor. Not one heart, though, but two small, eager organs joined like cherries with a stalk of artery. Cassy was there sometimes, pulling one of those slick and feeble hearts from its stem with her teeth like an animal at its afterbirth; swallowing it; feeling it beating inside her belly.

With the mornings, with consciousness, these dreams would fade. In periphery, in the last puffs of sleeping, they were remembered only by the uneasiness they left behind. Every morning Cassy would wake to an uncanny sense of loss, like the face of a childhood friend that memory couldn't quite conjure. Every morning she would wake before Adam with a name almost upon her lips. She let him sleep.

*

"You look tired," Adam said, looking into Cassy's dark eyes. "We can go another time."

She shushed him. "I told you I'd come. I want to come."

"You still not getting a decent night's sleep?" he asked. Above them the numbers on the station clocked changed and the milling crowd began to shuffle expectantly. He craned his neck down the track to see if he could spot their train and slipped his hand into hers. She let her head sag onto his shoulder and he said, "Rest on the train if you want."

The train journey seemed shorter to Adam this time. Perhaps because he was eager to share his news at his mother's graveside. He didn't want to keep Cassy in the cemetery too long, though. If she perked up a little he might suggest a stroll through the town or a pub lunch. If not he'd get her home nice and early.

Cassy tried to close her eyes but the rocking carriage dislodged too many thoughts and unsettled her. She made her excuses and stumbled down the lurching aisle to the toilets. In the chemical astringency of that small, swaying room she dry-retched a couple of times into the stainless steel bowl. Once they reached their stop she was glad to be on the solid platform and pulled in cold air in the hope that it might flush this uneasiness out of her system.

All the time she could see unspoken concern in Adam's eyes. She noticed each small scrutiny of her well-being and forced smiles to her lips and wished that she could settle herself for his sake.

She couldn't walk as fast as he, so it was a full half hour before they spotted the steeple between the houses, and the easy slope to that empty place wore her out. The nausea had gone, though. Adam tried the locked door to the church so that she might sit down inside but she said she would rather rest on the bench in the graveyard.

"I don't know if there is one" he said.

"There's always a bench," she said, and although she'd never been here before she knew there would be and old wooden seat underneath high, ivied railings before it came into view.

She sat with a loud exhalation, pulled her coat collar up, and watched Adam stroll through this silent garden towards his mother's plot. In his long coat, with his legs hidden behind headstones, he seemed to glide through the graveyard. She watched him briefly but felt like she was intruding upon something private, so instead she looked up at the white autumn sky. She traced the naked tree limbs and listened to the distant sounds of traffic. She wanted to go to his side, she wanted to see for herself, but it was calm where she was sitting and she was afraid of her dreams of this place.

She'd dreamt of this bench, this place. Adam had been here, at his mother's grave, but not to see her. She'd dreamt of him pulling the overgrowth away from the tiny headstone beside his mother's plot. It had been night-time in the dream but they'd both been able to read the worn inscription: Adam's birthday, the name Emma, and the fragment of poetry, taken – she knew this somehow – from a book that Adam's mother had studied when she had been at university. His twin sister's grave.

She watched him now, feet from the small plot which she knew was there. He was oblivious and she wouldn't have said a word to snatch that innocence from him now that he was finally happy.

In the dream he had been on his knees digging his fingers into the moist earth as drizzle patted his head and back with cold kisses. The sod which had lain between him and his sister for 19 years heaved upwards slightly.

Now he glanced over at her and she smiled. She saw him saying something to the ground and then he was gliding back towards her through the markers and stone memories, as though he was a ghost already and she had met him too late.

In her dream the wind had pushed the gathering rain into his face as he tore at the ground. The loneliness beneath him rose like a smell to greet him. He reached the tiny coffin. He clawed around the fragile wooden casket until he had enough purchase to lift the weightless load out, breathing heavily, feeling a throbbing from inside the box, wrenching the lid off and crying out.

"You hungry?" he called out to her and she shook her head.

There she had lain. Adam stood in the pit he'd dug and reverently curled his hands under his sister as if she were a kitten, then he lifted the tiny skeleton out of its coffin. The smell of freshly dug earth filled his nostrils and he cast the empty casket aside, then ever so slowly – as if he were trying not to wake her – he dropped to his knees, then onto one elbow, and then finally down onto his side. He held her close, curling himself around her as the rain began to fall in earnest, filling the hole in which they lay. The earth around them turned to mud and began to slide back over them, but he didn't care. He lay his head next to hers and closed his eyes.

"You look a little better," Adam said, dropping himself onto the bench beside her. She leaned across and kissed him lightly on the cheek. "Do you feel okay?"

For a time, in her dream, before the mud closed over them completely, Adam and his sister shared his heartbeat between them and were at peace.

"Do you feel okay?" he asked again, and Cassy nodded wanly.

He placed a light hand on her stomach, leaned conspiratorially towards it and whispered, "And what about you? Are you doing okay in there too?"

Cassy answered for the girl that grew inside her.

She knew it was a girl.

"I am."

AULD AGGIE

Everett Caulfield believed that you could get anything you wanted in life with the right lure. His father had taught him to fish, and what he'd taken away from those weekends was that the rivers and lakes of the Pacific Northwest contained thousands upon thousands of little mouths all searching for the next meal, and that if something looked tempting enough they'd take a bite.

Many years later in a therapy session Caulfield would recall a nature documentary he'd seen as a young boy. It was about the deep ocean, and it was the first time he'd seen an anglerfish. The ugly, bony sphere of a creature was mostly mouth and needle teeth. It had a long protuberance dangling from the centre of its head which it waggled back and forth in front of its mouth and the tip glowed like a firefly in the dark. He'd watched, both thrilled and appalled, as a smaller fish swam closer – curious, hungry – hoping that the glowing fancy might be its next meal. Then the giant mouth opened, sucking in the fish, and snapped shut over it with a finality that imprinted itself on his young mind.

What he came to realise was that it was not just fish which were constantly looking for something to grab onto. It was a world of bait and line and everybody was trying to catch the next meal and avoid a hook through the cheek. As he grew, Caulfield began to understand that lures could be ideas, or feelings, or promises. It got him a car for his graduation; it got him the girls he wanted at college; it got him the sales and promotions he desired at work and the life he wanted as a man. Until, of course, the one that got away.

She – his soon to be ex-wife – was playing on his mind when he booked the fishing trip to Scotland. He needed to get away for a couple of weeks. He rented a cottage on the shore of a western loch and spent his first couple of days on a beautiful little crescent of shingle a few hundred yards from his front door, casting into the still, deep waters.

He barely saw another soul and only the occasional boat powering its way across the glassy loch, leaving widening V-shaped wakes. It was a world away from selling real estate and his looming divorce. The air was crisp and still, and dark green mountains lay beyond the sparkling water like sleeping giants. There were only half a dozen cottages overlooking the loch, linked by one road which ran a couple of miles along the northern shore. His cottage stood at the end of that road, and the shingle beach lay beyond that, at the end of a rough dirt track.

On his first evening he sat on a foldaway seat in front of his cottage, drinking beer from a cooler as the sun sank behind the mountains to his right. A local passed by walking her scraggy little dog, maybe the fourth person he'd seen all day. She spied him and called out, "Mind the midges, they'll eat you alive!"

The second evening he decided to cycle the half hour to the nearest pub, The Water Horse. It was a low-ceilinged place full of gentle babble, like a simmering pot. His children would doubtless say the place was straight out of Lord of the Rings or a Harry Potter movie if they were here (or if they ever returned his calls).

Unlike the movies, thankfully, the conversation inside didn't stop when he entered, although he was certain that he'd instantly been marked as a tourist. When he ordered his first pint it was obvious that he was American. The barman asked him the usual small talk questions as he poured: Where are you from? Oregon. Where are you staying? I'm renting Croft Cottage by the loch. How long are you stopping for? I'm out here for two weeks, hoping to catch some fish. That caught the ear of some of the locals and drinks were bought and stories were swapped. They wanted to hear about the fishing in Oregon and were keen to offer advice about fishing the loch. Whisky chasers were added to the rounds and conversation was loose and amiable until a gruff old man at the bar butted in with: "You'll no be going out on the water, though. Especially not at night." It was a statement rather than a question.

"I'm sorry?" Caulfield said. The man had a ruddy face and a beard like the stiff bristles of an old broom. When he leaned forwards Caulfield could make out the broken blood vessels across his nose like tiny red curlicues.

"Auld Aggie might take a keek," he said.

There were some laughs, some scoffed, but others kept quiet.

"I'm sorry, I don't understand," Caulfield said.

"Auld Aggie is a wee bit of a legend in these parts," said Ewan, a middle-aged man with round apple cheeks. He and Caulfield had been discussing lures. "She's our very own lake monster."

"Less of the legend, I'll thank you," his mate, Doug, piped up.

"Oh yes, I was forgetting, you've seen her."

"Aye, moving across the loch one night as I was making my way home."

"Rat-arsed!" someone shouted and laughter broke out. Caulfield laughed along. The whisky had given him a jacket of contentment and a smile came to his lips more easily than it had in years.

"We, uh," he said, "we have a lake monster of our own in Oregon. He's called Wally. Because he lives in Wallowa Lake."

"That means something else here." More laughter.

Pints came freely and whisky followed. Caulfield shared details of his divorce – "Now there's a *real* monster" – and the locals shared their stories of scaly Auld Aggie.

By the time he left, Caulfield realised he wasn't steady enough on his bike to ride home, so he began walking, wheels clicking at his side, hoping that the bracing night air would sober him up a little.

The night was clear; there was no light pollution out here, so the stars of the Milky Way were loud as a trumpet blast across the sky. Beneath the stars the mountains hunkered black and brooding and the loch shone like mercury under the moon. He felt good; things would work out fine. This trip was exactly what he needed: a short break from lawyers, poisonous emails and screaming matches over the phone to get his head straight and get back in the game. He'd dangle the house and the cars in front of his wife and she'd snap them up and not bother to dig into his investments and the real money he had tucked away elsewhere. He felt unburdened as he wobbled his way home. Any time he glanced from the path to the glittering body of water he wondered if he'd see a slender neck, or a bulky body hauling itself ashore, or some humped shape slipping into the water from one of the tiny islands dotted here and there.

"Well, Aggie old girl, I'm about to be single," he slurred, then chuckled to himself. "Not that being married was ever a concern before."

He couldn't be sure if the locals in The Water Horse really believed all that bull or if they were just trying to wind up a dumb yank, but the more credulous he acted the more drinks they bought him, so in the end what did it really matter? By the time he reached the water's edge he felt clear-headed enough to get on the bicycle and took the last couple of miles at a rickety pace. He stumbled inside and up to bed and slept the dreamless sleep of the drunk.

The next morning he woke with a gasping thirst and a headache. Jesus, how much had he had to drink? *Those Scots sure can sink them,* he thought. He prowled down to the kitchen and while his coffee percolated he gulped two mouthfuls of water straight from the tap. He grimaced at the chalky taste. Through the kitchen window he could see there'd been a disturbance in the small front garden. He went out to investigate and was assaulted by the reek of fish. Half a salmon lay on his doorstep, jelly-eyed and mouth agape. Flies were already congregating around the pale, chummy guts which spilled from its torn body. The tap water in his empty stomach churned and threatened to come back up as he stepped barefoot over the fish.

The front garden was little more than a postage stamp of grass. There was kelp strewn here and there and gouges had been taken out of the lawn. As he turned to survey the damage he finally saw the three deep furrows scored into the front door as well.

Those sons of bitches.

He navigated the stinking fish head again to retrieve his phone, then set about taking photos and video evidence of the vandalism.

So, they thought it would be fun to prank the tourist, huh? Loosen me up and regale me with stories of the local beast, then when I'm sleeping pull this trick-or-treat shit?

He remembered sharing his marriage woes with them and the sting of embarrassment burned into indignation. He'd talked to them about his damned kids, and they were laughing behind his back, trying to scare him off the water with some bugaboo fairy tales.

At first he intended to call the police, but while he showered and dressed his anger simmered. The early nausea of his hangover had turned into deep hunger, so he cooked a large breakfast and forked it into his mouth at the dining room table with his laptop open next to him. He googled "Auld Aggie" and as he ate he read the legends and the recorded sightings, marrying some accounts to the stories he'd been told in The Water Horse the night before.

It was all bullshit. Every significant body of water across the globe had a monster or a spirit. Every single one. He'd grown up with the tales of his own lake monster. If the water out there had anything in it then folks were likely seeing catfish. Those brutes could reach hundreds of pounds and grow almost as long as a man. Unexpecting eyes might easily mistake their flat brown heads and wide, whiskered mouths just below the surface for a monster. If not catfish, then a giant sturgeon; or at a push Aggie might be a succession of giant eels spotted over the years. They were born sterile and didn't feel the pull to spawn, so when the rest of their kin left the lakes and rivers of Europe to go and mate in the Sargasso Sea, they stayed in the freshwater. They stayed, and ate, and grew. Really grew. Those were your serpents.

By the time Caulfield had finished his breakfast his simmering rage had turned cold. He wasn't going to call the police; what would the local bobby do anyway? He was going to take a rowboat out onto the loch tonight and he was going to catch "Auld Aggie", or whatever passed for her.

He drove to the nearest town and picked up some supplies: food, stronger rods, and the right bait. Back at the cottage he looked over the rowboat which came with the holiday home with a cold efficiency. He had a late lunch and read through the accounts of Auld Aggie again; the exaggeration; the self-publicising; taking perfectly natural phenomena and inflating them into something special because that made the witness special. And doubtless the people of the area weren't too quick to dismiss the sightings and the legends because that made them special too. He knew how all of this worked. But they'd jabbed at him. They'd taken him for a fool, and so now he was going to pull the thing that made them special out of the lake — a monstrous fish, no doubt, but no monster. He was going to drag it ashore and gut it and show those who'd laughed at him just how ordinary they were.

He put together some provisions, ate a light supper, then loaded the boat just as evening was setting in and the midges hovered at the water's edge in fine clouds. The boat creaked a little as he pulled on the oars, taking it out into deeper water. A breeze thrilled the surface into a broad shiver of wavelets and soon all he could hear was the water against the side of the boat, his own exercised breathing, and the occasional distant call of some unidentified bird.

The moon was already in the sky, a pale face at the window, and the sun was making its way home behind the mountains when he made his first cast.

He settled into the slow rhythm of the sport. Water lapped around him, the sky darkened and the half-moon got brighter. Back on shore sparse points of light flicked on and slowly multiplied. Caulfield scowled at them. He was certain those who'd pranked him had noted him out on the loch and he was sure that by now they were sat in The Water Horse laughing at him.

Screw 'em.

He cast again. His bait made a tiny splash as it hit the water and sent ripples out across the still surface of the loch. Shadows lengthened. Whenever he got a bite then everything else but him, the line, and the fish melted away. He danced with them, let them run, tired them out and reeled them in. He caught some impressive specimens too, but none were what he was after, so he landed them, pulled the hooks from their faces, and tossed them back in. He was getting his hand and eye in, though; he was warming to the quarry which he knew was out there. It had probably already marked him. It may even have come sniffing and passed underneath him. It would bite eventually.

The bait stank and occasionally his fingers would get oily. He dipped them in the cold water and wiped them on his trousers. A red glow lingered in the sky long after the sun went behind the mountains, but eventually that too faded and the stars had their time. The glow of the moon intensified and turned the lake into ripples of black and silver.

Again and again he cast into the loch and the little plop of bait hitting water came back to him, and the lapping of water on wood, and every once in a while a splash – sometimes distant, sometimes nearby – of something breaching the surface and sending silver rings out through the ink. The boat creaked and the nearby islands of the loch breached the water, hunched like the humps of some giant creature's back. Caulfield wasn't prone to poetic thinking, but out on the water, alone and in the dark, the accounts of the sightings played on his mind.

In 1972 on a bright autumn morning Travis Wilson was out on his boat. The water was calm and he was halfway across the loch when he approached what he thought was a man standing up in a boat. As he got closer he saw that it was actually a long, snake-like neck standing out of the water by about five or six feet. He quickly changed tack, and as he sailed away the dark shape dropped unhurriedly back beneath the surface.

A stray cloud passed over the moon and everything got darker. The sound of the water around the rowboat seemed louder in the brief gloom. Something splashed nearby as he reeled in his bait at a steady pace.

In July 1985 a picnicking family on the southern shore of the loch noticed a patch of water which frothed and trembled maybe 20 or 30 yards from shore on an otherwise glassy surface. There was no wind. As they watched, the disturbance moved rapidly out to deeper waters. They observed it zig-zagging across the loch for eight minutes before it disappeared.

A swell from somewhere out in the darkness rocked him. The wake from a passing boat, perhaps, although he hadn't seen or heard any other craft on the water since sunset. Something going at speed could send out waves for quite a distance, though; he might not have spotted it.

In May 2001 a couple – Bobby and Margret Milne – were driving across the short span of river where it leaves the loch and makes its way to the sea. Near the mouth of the loch the river flows over a gravel bar, so that for a short distance it is only a few feet deep. Margaret saw a large, powerful animal lurching across the gravel there and called for her husband to stop the car. He did so in time for them both to see a bulky shape heaving itself into the deep waters of the loch. Bobby recalled the sense of power from the muscular hindquarters as it pushed itself over the ridge.

Something yanked at the bait and Caulfield had to grip tightly onto his rod as vibrations went up his forearms. He held fast and let the line play out. Something was running fast with the bait. This could be it. Then from behind came another swell, larger than the first, and the boat rolled, sending him off kilter. He threw out an arm for balance and the rod flew out of his hand. He crouched, riding the swell until he could lower himself back down onto his seat and grab the sides of the boat.

The water was agitated all around him and the boat was turning lazily anti-clockwise. He lost his orientation and snapped his head around as the boat span, trying to get a bearing on the northern shore and Croft Cottage. Something scraped across the underside of the boat – surely a piece of wood or some other debris floating around on the water, he thought. After a few seconds the scraping noise stopped, the swell subsided, and the boat settled back onto an even keel, still slowly turning. Everything was calm once again. Caulfield cursed his lost rod and whatever detritus had got snagged on the underside of the boat.

He had a spare rod and had to decide now whether to carry on or row back to shore. He was certain whatever had taken the bait was the fish he wanted to catch. If the hook was properly set then his sinking rod would drag it deeper and he wouldn't get it to bite again. He was a little agitated by the sudden commotion on the water and admitted as much to himself. He'd let himself get spooked.

He was further out towards the middle of the loch now, near one of the small islands, and the lights of the northern shore looked like a string of fairy lights. The thought of hauling his ass all the way back there empty-handed stung. He imagined the patrons of The Water Horse asking how his spot of night fishing had gone. He imagined them smirking, asking if he'd seen Aggie, and his anger was back at the surface again, hot and sharp.

He reached for his second rod, tied off the line and baited his hook. Before he could even cast off there came the sound of splashing water again, off to his left. The moonlight played on a disturbed surface maybe 100 yards away. The disturbance turned into a swell and that dark bulge of water moved towards his boat, closing the distance at pace. He couldn't fathom what he was seeing. It would reach the boat in seconds. Another cloud passed in front of the moon as the rushing sound of water got closer. This was all wrong. There was nothing in the lake. It must be some natural phenomena. The wave was almost upon him and despite his denials his brain was already preparing him to run, squirting adrenaline into his bloodstream and sending oxygen to his muscles. He yelled and held his rod out uselessly as if it were a talisman. Did he see a dark shape beneath the surging water? It would hit the boat at any moment. All rationality left him; the oncoming water sounded like a train and there was a scream in his head, a primate call of danger, urging flight. He felt the stern of the rowboat rising and without another thought he jumped.

He hit the water and the sudden shock of cold shut out everything else for a second. He began pulling through the waves, thrashing his arms ahead of him, swallowing water, unsure if he heard the smashing of his boat over the sound of his own splashing or if he imagined it. He'd lost all bearings. Clouds hung over the moon and the night was dark above him and the deep loch black beneath him. As he spluttered and struggled he caught a glimpse of a light. There must be someone else out on the water, someone who'd heard his distress and had come to help.

He swam towards it but after about ten strokes realised that he was swimming towards a large, dark mass looming out of the water. It took him a few panicked heartbeats to realise that it was the nearby island, not some creature rearing from the water. The strange tides out on the loch had brought him much closer to the island than he'd realised, and there was a light there, through the trees. He swam with a purpose now and when he reached the muddied banks he pulled himself up on hands and knees, slipping and scrabbling for dry land.

He rose on unsteady legs and turned to face the water. He scanned the loch but couldn't see his boat or any debris on the water. There was no disturbance, no ripples, no wakes. He was breathing heavily, shivering, and his sodden clothes were heavy. He was grateful for the welcome, warm blob of light shining beyond the trees somewhere towards the centre of this hump of land. He set off towards it, exhausted.

The island wasn't particularly large, about a dozen acres at best. He thrashed through undergrowth and around trees and eventually reached the source of the light. It as a wood cabin set in a clearing. The glow was coming from inside, perhaps firelight. He stumbled into the clearing.

"Hello," he called. The cabin was squat and long and by the woozy light of the moon he could see that the front door was open. The golden light inside moved past one of the windows and towards the door as he approached.

"Hello," he called again, "I need help."

A figure appeared at the door. A stout young woman holding a lantern. She stood in the doorway and regarded him silently.

"I'm sorry to disturb you," Caulfield said, teeth chattering now. "I capsized… out on the loch," he added redundantly. "I didn't know anyone lived on these islands. I didn't mean to frighten you. Can you help me?" She was holding the lantern up by her face and he squinted against the light, unable to make out her features. He approached and she backed inside wordlessly. He wondered if this woman lived some kind of hermit life out here. She certainly wouldn't expect a soaking wet stranger to come crashing through the bushes towards her home. He had no choice, though, he needed her help and he needed to get warm.

He climbed onto the wooden porch and stepped inside. This strange, silent woman had moved back to the far end of the cabin. She held the lantern just beneath her chin and he squinted again to try and make out her features. The inside of the cabin was sparse and undecorated.

"It's alright," he said, "don't be afraid."

He moved towards her and wobbled. The floor had a pronounced slant down towards the back of the cabin. It was slick, too. His feet slipped out from under him and he fell hard on his backside and slid across the floor a couple of feet. He grunted and tried to push himself back up. There was a kind of slime across the floor and as he rolled over his hands slid away from him through that gunk.

"What? I can't —" he said, struggling to get upright, sliding further down the canted floor for his efforts. The place smelt of bile and rotting fish; it stung his nostrils and he could taste it in the back of his throat.

"Help," he said to the woman. The light from her lantern was dimming, and before it was extinguished completely he saw that her face was a putty of almost features and her hair was a mass of kelp, not a woman at all. Closer now, he saw that the lantern was just the bulbous end of one of those imitation arms, glowing but fading.

Caulfield rolled over onto his front and tried to crawl back up the incline to the door, but there was no purchase and he kept sliding back down. The open doorway was the only source of light now, a rectangle of gentle blue moonlight. In that half-light he saw that the walls of the cabin had become slick and they were pulsating. Wet sounds came from behind him. He kicked his legs frantically and clawed at the slimy, tilted floor which seemed to turn spongy. His panting sounded hot and close;

the echoes of his cries were dampened in this porous space.

The rectangle of doorway stretched and widened, becoming much wider than it was tall. Then, slowly, it began to close, the top coming down like a garage door. The last thing Everett Caulfield noticed before it shut out the light completely was that it was full of teeth.

THE KICKABOUT

The day of this year's kickabout had come. Lazy summer heat stretched out the afternoon like toffee while Michael sat on his jumper by the side of the shabby field. His younger brother, Heath, was off in the tickling, tall grass, trying to catch the grasshoppers which filled the air with their raucous, sawing conversation. They'd been out of school for weeks already, but the holidays still seemed to reach on to the horizon.

Two other boys were running, scrape-kneed, around the middle of the field, flinging small stones at one another. Michael wanted to join their noisy stone war, but he was mindful of his promise to look after his little brother. Behind him Heath was giggling, far too clumsy to ever catch one of the lively insects he was stalking. Other boys were arriving now, stomping across the unkempt patch of land. This year's kickabout would be starting soon, they just needed Peter Prentiss to arrive with the ball.

As usual the plans for this year's game had spread through word of mouth – strictly no DMs, WhatsApp messages or social media of any kind.

Michael had been told the date, place, and time on the last day of school as he was moving through a busy corridor between classes.

"Who's been picked to bring the ball?" he'd asked in an urgent whisper. The answer had surprised him. Peter Prentiss was in the same year as him, although they were not friends. Prentiss hadn't joined the kickabout in previous years, nor had he ever shown any interest in normal games, either in or out of school. He was a sallow boy who kept to himself and spent a lot of time in the Music Room during break. Michael heard that Peter Prentiss played the trumpet or violin or something, and he practised while everyone else was outside running and hollering.

"Hey, loser," he called over his shoulder to Heath, who ignored him. "Loser!"

"I'm *not* a loser!"

"Come here, I've got something to tell you."

"I'm not a loser," Heath said, sulking now.

"This is important," Michael said. "I'll help you catch a grasshopper after the game," he lied. Heath came sullenly to his side as another pair of boys – no, three of them – squeezed through the gap in the chain-link fence at the bottom of the field. They were older boys with flinty faces. They had studded boots slung around their necks, dangling by the knotted laces.

"Listen, the kickabout's going to begin soon. It can get pretty rough, so I want you to stay off to the side here and guard our jumpers, okay?"

"I want to play," Heath said.

"No, you can't play. It's a bigger boys' game. But you can watch, and you can guard the jumpers. It won't take long, then we can do whatever you want for the rest of the day. How does that sound?" Heath pursed his lips in thought before agreeing with a small "Okay."

The sun began a languorous descent, taking a little of the heat out of the air. A light breeze spoke of a chill to come, but the day was still warm enough. Michael was surprised to see quite how many boys were beginning to congregate; news of the kickabout must have spread further this year, some of these boys were from adjoining towns.

A loose circle was forming around the ill-defined edges of the playing area. He spotted a couple of his friends, Ali and Jamie, and sauntered over to chat to them with Heath in tow. Some of the older kids were setting up goalposts out of mounds of clothes at either end of the field. Sides were being assigned. There were scuffles here and there with voices raised in argument or horseplay. Boys began to crane their necks and look around like animals on the savanna, impatient for the arrival of Peter Prentiss and the ball.

"Prentiss wouldn't back out, would he?" said Jamie.

"No," Michael said, the very thought shocking. "He wanted to play so he can stick to the rules like everyone else. He has to bring the ball and he knows what'll happen if he doesn't show up."

"Why's he playing anyway?" Jamie said. "He's gonna get his shins kicked to shreds."

"Perhaps he wants to fit in?" Michael said with a shrug.

"I think he's chickened out," Ali said, stabbing at a tuft of dry grass with the toe of his boot. Michael looked down at Heath with a twinge of guilt. He shouldn't have brought him.

"Hey," he said, crouching to get his brother's attention. "The big boys can get rough. When the game starts I want you to stand off to the side over there, okay?" The grasshoppers no longer chirped in the long grass. "Hey, Heath. Do you remember when we found that cat which had been run over?" Heath nodded uncertainly. "You got pretty upset, which is okay. Well, I don't want you to get upset today. You don't have to watch the game if you don't want to, but if you're with the big boys then you have to act like a big boy, understand? No crying, and most important of all no telling mummy and daddy." Heath began to pull at his bottom lip, a holdover from when he still sucked his thumb. Bringing him had been a mistake, but he couldn't back out; he'd put his name down; those were the rules.

The mood grew testy as the sun got lower. There were murmurs in the crowd, like ripples on water when something large moves just beneath the surface. Heath was getting bored and fussy and it was becoming harder for Michael to make him keep still.

There was a pinkish tinge to the western horizon by the time Peter Prentiss struggled through the chain-link fence and stumbled across the field with an awkward sack; no, not a sack but a pillowcase. He was met with jeers and name calling, and when he got nearer it was clear that he had been crying. The gathered crowd encircled him and Peter Prentiss was visibly on the verge of tears again.

"Where the fuck have you been?" a boy with the beginnings of a wispy moustache said.

"I couldn't find anything. I looked and looked, but I couldn't find anything." Prentiss was struggling with the pillowcase and laid the lumpy weight down at his feet gently. Something inside moved and began to mewl.

"Fuck sake, you've had weeks to get ready," the boy with the peach fuzz lip said. "We gave you the traps and bait. You've got neighbours with pets."

"I couldn't find anything," Prentiss said again. Michael saw his bottom lip wobbling and felt a little sick because he knew that the boy was going to blub again. "I looked all over. I set the bait every night." The contents of the pillowcase began to kick more vigorously and the mewling within became a cry. One of the boys reached down and pulled the pillowcase up by its corner, emptying the contents out onto the dry grass.

"I had to wait till my mam took her afternoon nap," Prentiss was sobbing now. "I had to wait till she was asleep."

Some boys pushed him aside where he continued to bawl, all snot and tears. On the ground Peter's baby brother cried in tandem with him. Both the Prentiss boys wailed into the torpid summer sky. The gathered players looked down at the red-faced bundle in silence. Michael urgently motioned for Heath to step back, much further back.

"Play on!" someone shouted, and that year's kickabout was underway.

THE DEATH OF DESIRE

As is often the case, it was the smell which first alerted someone to the body. The police were called to the west London lock up and had to break in. What they found inside… well.

Sally Jessop was a coroner's officer; she investigated unexplained or unnatural deaths to help the coroner determine when, how, and why somebody died. She tried her best not to take her work home with her, but you wouldn't be human if some cases didn't affect you. Sally always had a tougher time with the elderly people who died alone with no family, and the young suicides whose families were burdened with questions they might never be able to answer. This case hit her in a different and unexpected way, though. She became fascinated by it. It was the "why" of this one which persisted like a steady drip and seemed to leech the colour from the other areas of her life. She couldn't stop thinking about the death of this young man, a man whose life she'd spent the last few days scrutinising.

His name was Andrew Harcourt and he was 23 when he died. He had no living relatives and no real friends as far as she could glean. He'd been an artist, and Sally got the dispiriting feeling that she'd spent more time looking at his art this week than anyone else ever had. She couldn't tell if he had any promise, but some of his pieces left her with a lingering feeling she couldn't quite define, especially the few bits of video work she'd found on a neglected YouTube channel he'd set up some years ago; work with single digit and sometimes no views until she'd found them.

The lock up he'd been renting had been padlocked from the inside. When the police forced their way in they'd found his body in a fairly advanced state of decomposition. They called the coroner's office and Tom had attended in his hazmat suit with a digital camera to document the scene and collect the decedent.

Sally thought of Tom's photos: the view from outside the lock up, looking in; Andrew Harcourt in the middle of the sparse space on a folding metal chair with his back to the shutter doors, slumped forward and to one side, but not enough to topple him from his seat. Then the pictures crept closer, recording the young man from all angles. The flies had found him. He was sitting facing an old looking camcorder on a tripod; in the corner of the room was a trestle table with some brushes, pens and sketch paper (but no note). Next to the table a small beer fridge contained some supermarket sandwiches and a bottle of orange juice (both unopened). Tom had photographed it all. When the results of the post-mortem examination had come back from the forensic pathologist those were the images which haunted Sally the most — that food and drink untouched, just a few steps from the chair Andrew Harcourt had died in.

She rubbed her eyes against the glow of her laptop as she sat in bed. It was already five past midnight and she'd found her way to his YouTube channel again like a dog returning to vomit. It was called 'Andrew Harcourt Art'. She thought about that camcorder on the tripod facing his discoloured, bloated body, and her finger hovered over the touchpad before clicking once again on a video called 'The Death of Desire.' She'd already watched it five times in the last three days.

The video was black and white, low definition, and started with a handheld shot from the ground looking up at a residential tower block. She couldn't identify the building and it wasn't named in the video description. Clouds were scudding through the sky behind the tower, and then the camera made its way inside. The video was a continuous shot and took the viewer up the winding concrete staircase, up to one of the uppermost floors where it approached the balcony — providing a brief shot of an anonymous skyline — and then tumbled over the edge, falling to the same spot on the ground where it had begun. For a few moments the frame was filled with a lopsided view of the ground as the camera lay on its side, and then it rose, looked back up at the building — same clouds rushing by – before entering again and climbing the stairs.

It was a loop, but no matter how many times she watched it at various speeds Sally couldn't tell how it had been filmed or where the beginning and end of the footage had been spliced together.

The loop – the journey from the ground, up the repeating stairs, off the balcony and back down – took four minutes and twenty-six seconds, but the entire uploaded video ran for almost ten hours. Sally had jumped around along the time bar to see if the footage changed, but it was always this Sisyphean repetition.

This wasn't the video she really wanted to watch; it wasn't the last video Andrew Harcourt had recorded; that was at work. She'd seriously considered making a copy and bringing it home to watch, despite how deeply unethical and morbid that would have been. A breach like that would almost certainly get her fired. Yet in the last three days, while she had been compiling her report for the coroner, she had watched it at her desk seventeen times, checking over her shoulder to ensure none of her colleagues had noticed this growing compulsion.

She let out a big sigh. This wasn't like her at all. She closed her laptop and padded out into the hall so she could have a quick wee before trying to get some much-needed sleep. There was a dim light downstairs coming from the kitchen. She went down to investigate and found her teenage daughter, Leah, standing in front of the fridge. She was holding the door open, washed in cold light, staring at the contents. She didn't move or make any sign that she noticed her mother's presence.

"Leah?" Sally said.

Leah was still for a few seconds then seemed to rouse, as if waking from a nap.

"Oh, hi Mum," she said.

"Are you hungry? It's late."

"Mmm?" Leah seemed a little dazed. "No, I'm not hungry," she said and closed the refrigerator door. She turned and left, her slippers scuffing across the lino, and Sally watched her as she shuffled back upstairs to her room. Sally followed, went to the loo, then took herself back to bed.

With sleep came dreams.

She couldn't remember her dreams the next day, but they cast a drab pall over the morning. In a rush as usual, she packed a lunch which Leah was unlikely to touch, then harried her daughter off her phone and hurried her off to school, leaving just enough time for her to chomp some toast as she brushed her hair and searched for her keys.

At work she appraised her cases listlessly. She was thinking of only one.

With any unexplained death the forensic pathologist looks for obvious signs of injury before moving to an internal examination. Andrew Harcourt had locked himself into that small space. The key was in his pocket. He'd been alone. There were no outward signs of trauma and no disease or damage internally. Sally brought up the results of the post-mortem examination again, although she knew the contents. She flitted to the part which said there had been no stomach contents or faecal matter in his bowels, and signs of severe dehydration and malnutrition.

She flicked back to Tom's photos and found the ones which showed the contents of that small beer fridge – a packet of chicken and mayo sandwiches and a bottle of smooth orange juice. Tom had taken pictures of the "use by" dates of both items. Such things could be used to help determine a rough time of death. They'd both expired about two weeks before Andrew had been found.

And here was the toxicology report. She had expected indications of an overdose of some kind. There were none.

Luckily they had the video.

Sally paused before playing it again, perhaps so that she could pretend she had a choice. The icon sat there on her desktop, her little cursor arrow over it. She'd known from the moment she woke this morning that she was going to watch it again. She clicked on it.

Andrew Harcourt had set his camcorder up to face the folding chair beneath the bare bulb hanging from the ceiling. He'd used a time lapse setting so that it took one image every 30 seconds. He'd started recording, then sat down in the chair.

It had taken some time for the police to stitch together the images into a watchable film, and when Sally played the file the familiar interior of the lock up filled the screen. Time moved swiftly on the video; every ten seconds of film was about two hours of real time. The whole video lasted almost 15 minutes, and over the course of that time almost a week passed inside the lock up. A bar of light beneath the shutter door slowly strobed on and off denoting the passage of day and night outside, otherwise the only thing to move in the video was the young man himself. He sat upright in the chair but seemed to blur and buzz as time sped up – he jerked and vibrated in the seat but never left it and never took his eyes from the camera.

Sally watched him speeding towards his death one more time and the sounds of her colleagues on the phone to the police, bereaved families, and doctor's surgeries dissolved into a hum, and it felt as if Andrew Harcourt's reverberating body was making that sound.

Time charged on in the video and there were periods of seconds where he'd clearly fallen asleep in the chair, and just as rapidly he was awake again but fast becoming more sluggish with each passing day, sometimes looking as if he was being rattled by spasms, skin greying, but never leaving the chair.

On the fourth day he slumped forwards and to the side and the image of him settled for a while. The bar of light pulsed beneath the door, his skin began to darken, then the flies arrived, bursting around him like time-lapsed static on the picture as he began to swell and quickly decompose.

The shock she'd felt the first time she watched the video had long since subsided. Now each time she watched it she simply felt a little hollower. As it played she would feel a growing tug in the pit of her stomach, and those 15 minutes seemed to lurch on forever, but every time the video ended she felt as if it had finished too quickly and had to resist the compulsion to play it again.

She would be surprised if the coroner ruled that he intended to take his own life. There was simply not enough strong evidence to show intention in that way. Most likely Andrew Harcourt's death would be recorded as a tragic accident; the creation of an art piece involving extreme fasting which had been pushed too far. Sally couldn't shake a nagging doubt, though. It was perhaps the intensity with which he'd stared at the camera on that first day as if daring her to watch, challenging her to look away. And that food and drink only a few feet away, with him showing no intention of leaving that chair.

Sally wondered if this, the full video, all of it, was meant to be his final piece of art. If that was the case then only a pathetically small number of people would ever see it. In some perverse way, although she didn't particularly like the art he'd produced, the fact that she'd watched it so many times made her his biggest admirer.

She would wrap up her report and pass her findings and thoughts to the coroner this afternoon, then it would be out of her hands. She would resist the urge to copy this file and she would never watch that video again. She also made a promise to herself that she would never visit 'Andrew Harcourt Art' again. If she began taking her work home with her like this then she might end up as a case on somebody else's desk. It was a harsh thing to think, but whatever his intention was, like so many others, Andrew Harcourt was just another failed artist.

That evening she cooked dinner for her and Leah without much enthusiasm. She had to call up the stairs three times for her daughter to come and eat, and eventually Leah came down and sat with her in silence, glued to her phone.

"Put your phone down," she said.

Leah sucked her teeth and Sally repeated her command with a little more force.

"Oh, mum, I can't miss this," Leah said.

"What is so important?" she asked.

"It's all over the internet. It's mad. Some kind of stunt or trick. This girl's been livestreaming from her flat twenty-four seven; she hasn't moved, hasn't spoken, and right now two million people are watching her. There are mad conspiracy theories floating around about it. This is her third day, they reckon."

They fell into silence.

Leah didn't even pick up her fork.

Eventually the food got cold but Sally didn't bother to clear it away. She just sat in her seat and stared at it, unmoving.

THE LAPWING'S DECREE

In all the excitement of a new guest – a businessman from London, no less – Mrs Tavistock forgot her manners. She showed Mr Barker up to his room, took her leave, and was halfway downstairs before she realised she hadn't told him about breakfast. She climbed the creaking stairs once again and entered his room without knocking. On such small hooks are the tapestries of Hell's infernal plan hung.

She bridled when she found him bent down and fussing with the bed skirts. She prided herself on her bedmaking; her corners were hospital perfect.

"Is everything to your satisfaction?" she asked.

Mr Barker flushed and straightened.

"I, er..." he coughed an embarrassed laugh. With his jacket off his shirt and tie billowed around his thin frame like galleon sails. The cuffs were frayed. In this moment he looked like a boy playing dress up. "You caught me," he said. Her stare was straight as a pin. "Whenever I stay in a new room I always check under the bed for, uh... for monsters." A blast of briny coastal air filled the room through the open sash window. In the distance seabirds shouted throaty orders. "Ever since I was a child," Mr Barker continued. "I can't shake the habit."

"Well," Mrs Tavistock said, unsure how to reply, "I forgot to tell you that I serve breakfast between seven and nine. I have a good selection of canned goods in just now. I'll leave you in peace."

She paused at the door to cast a final eye around the room and stood in a spot of diffused afternoon sunlight. Mr Barker saw, with relief, that the light washed away her years and for the space of a passing cloud she looked young again. He was glad. Sometimes the faces went the other way and he saw people as they would end up, bloated and worm ridden.

"Seven. I look forward to it," he said. She moved out of the shaft of light and was suddenly old again.

Mr Barker listened to the seconds of silence as she paused on the other side of the door and then to her receding pigeon steps on threadbare carpet. He let out air like a puncture and moved to the open window.

He'd never seen the sea before, so when he'd received instructions to make his way to the south coast he thought he might finally get a chance to see the edge of the world. The journey south had been tough. No cars anymore, of course, and he'd been instructed to avoid the horse drawn coaches and trap services which were springing up to reconnect parts of the country. Instead he'd secured a bicycle by his usual means and slept under the stars, but a flat tyre had forced him to make the final miles on foot.

Still, the closer he got to the coast the more the road dipped downwards and he was able to pretend for an hour or two that he really was a businessman on his holidays. This bed and breakfast room did not afford him a sea view, but he could smell it in the air now, and he could hear it in the distance like a great hand stirring stones.

Mr Barker wasn't his real name. It wasn't even the name of the man who had previously owned this suit. It was a name he'd taken from the spine of a book he'd found mouldering in an abandoned house in Stepney. He fell back onto the bed with a squeal of springs.

"She's gone," he said in a flat voice.

The Seagull waddled out from underneath the pink valance and cocked its neck at him, squinting through a furnace-black eye. It shook itself, ruffling its mangy feathers and clapping its beak at him. The large bird scraped its leathery feet across the thin carpet towards the window and with a couple of angry flaps hauled itself onto the nightstand beside the bed. He tried to ignore it as it preened itself but the bird waited until he eventually looked its way, then it pirouetted on the nightstand, lifted its tail like a fan and shat on the carpet. It hopped onto the windowsill, eyed him pointedly one final time, then flew away.

Mr Barker lay in silence. In the bathroom a tap was dripping. The Seagull would return soon with details of the job. At least it hadn't started talking yet.

*

At breakfast Mr Barker forced himself to eat at a respectable pace. He was supposed to be on holiday, after all. Everything must look normal.

The dining area was set in a conservatory at the back of the building. Gentle morning drizzle pattered against the glass panes like little feet, whilst slightly warped big band music played from a wind-up radio in the corner. Someone was broadcasting down in the south, then.

Mrs Tavistock practically waltzed between the tables, dizzy at the opportunity to tend to guests. He imagined that even when the place was empty she would make up the beds, hang the towels, put lavender pouches in the drawers and move from table to table, humming to herself like a dying bee, setting napkins and cutlery and adjusting doilies. Now, though, she had two real guests, and Mr Barker had been surprised to find that he was not the only resident when he came down for breakfast.

A young lady sat three tables away, eating tinned fruit cocktail with a silver fork. He'd instantly dropped his gaze when he saw her and now only snatched sideways glances at her. Her hair was blonde and straight, down to her shoulders, and she dipped her head to meet her fork as she ate. Mr Barker strained to listen whenever Mrs Tavistock glided past her table with a comment, but she was so softly spoken that he couldn't make out anything she said. He tried to concentrate on his tin of baked beans with pork sausages, dissecting each small sausage into conservative pieces. He tried to ignore the thick red smear of ketchup at the side of the plate. It made him think of his last job.

Mrs Tavistock moved around the empty tables and approached him as the radio began to play "Pennsylvania 6-5000". Mr Barker was grateful for the spotty rain which smudged the light inside and kept her face fixed as she neared.

"Is everything to your satisfaction, Mr Barker?" she was beaming.

He nodded and swallowed. He'd done his tie up too tight and it was pinching his throat. Mrs Tavistock leaned in conspiratorially and stage whispered, "I have another tin of fruit cocktail in the pantry if you'd like something sweet for afters." He pushed a smile onto his face and dabbed the bean juice at the corners of his mouth with his napkin.

"Yes please," he said, "that would be delightful." He couldn't remember the last time he'd eaten fruit. One of the molars in the back of his mouth had been aching for weeks now and he was sure it was getting looser.

"Delightful," Mrs Tavistock echoed as if she were testing the quality of the word like struck crystal. At that moment the rain stopped and the sun came out, lighting her hair like a wispy halo and bleaching away her years in an instant. Mr Barker saw that in her youth she'd looked very much like the young lady at the other table who was now rising from her seat.

"Thank you very much for breakfast, it was delicious" she said in a small voice, a fist raised to her mouth as she spoke. She had to pass near his own table to leave and he dropped his eyes to his plate, fearful that the sudden sunlight would turn her face into whatever swollen worm food was eventually in store for her.

"Was everything satisfactory, Ms Pointer?" Mrs Tavistock asked as she walked her guest out of the conservatory. He couldn't make out the softly spoken reply. He watched the back of Ms Pointer's head as they left. His pulse was up and he felt this dead man's suit on him like a skin in need of sloughing. When he was alone he stood and paced cautiously around the bare tables until he stood behind Ms Pointer's vacated seat, then he laid a hand lightly over her fork, placing his fingers where hers had been minutes before.

"Ms Pointer," he murmured quietly to himself.

*

Back in his room the Seagull was waiting for him, even though he couldn't remember leaving the window open. It was sitting on the nightstand. He quietly pushed the door closed and stood in the middle of the room. The bird reeked. Its yellow beak ended in a cruel hook.

"You got any smokes?" it said in a guttural voice which smelled of fish. The pit of Mr Barker's stomach churned. That always happened now when they spoke. "C'mon, be a pal," the bird wheedled, its words coming like burps, "this sea air is killin' me."

Mr Barker fished around in his jacket pockets and extracted a crumpled packet of cigarettes.

"Atta boy!" the bird cawed as he lit one, approached carefully and placed it at arm's length in the snapping beak. "Ya know," it said, pausing to take the offering, "they told me that you'd be difficult to work with, but I think we're gonna get this job done just fine."

"They have a job?" Mr Barker said. "Is it?..."

"Wet?" the bird's wings shivered, "Oh, it's as wet as wet can be, my friend. Order comes straight from the Lapwing. You can go *paddling* in this one if you so desire." Mr Barker's gorge rose and he struggled to swallow it down without being too obvious about it.

"Who?" he managed to whisper.

"Some broad," the gull's chest puffed, "you met her downstairs. Name of Pointer. The Parliament wants her out of the way and they need it done before she leaves this place." Mr Barker's face flushed; he tried to hide it but the bird's black pearl of an eye saw everything. It hopped off the nightstand and flapped clumsily onto the bed, dropping ash on the duvet. It spread its wings out in resignation and muttered, "I know, I know, it's a shame, she's a looker. The Lapwing was insistent, however." It waddled to the end of the bed, springs squeaking as it went. "Listen, pal, I was told what went down in Edinburgh and I get it, I really do. You don't like doing the dames. But like I say, the Lapwing was *insistent*. I'm here to make sure your prick doesn't get between you and the job. Mark my words, if I think that's a possibility then I'll rip it off. But hey," it said in a lighter tone, creasing its wings into a little shrug, "maybe if you do this thing right I'll let you fuck her after."

*

As soon as the Seagull left through the window he had to get outside. The room felt like a coffin and he wanted to breathe salty air, see the sea, and feel its spray on his face.

The light rain from earlier cast a sheen on the cobbles and slate roofs of the small fishing town and filled the air with the slimy smell of kelp. The roads were narrow and twisty, with buildings packed in on either side. No road or pavement seemed to be flat but undulated as if in sympathy with the sea, which this place clung to like a barnacle. He tried following his feet downhill, assuming those roads would eventually lead to the shore, but even though the sound of the surf got louder sometimes, he could never quite find his way out of the streets and onto a dock or a pebbled beach.

The roads were quiet, but there had to be others still living here, he thought. The flu had done its brutal work, but there were still cities and towns and pockets of people everywhere. It couldn't just be Mrs Tavistock here all alone in her bed and breakfast, dithering the days away on guests real or imagined. Assuming, of course, that it *was* her B&B – she may have simply moved in one day and decided to stay and play landlady. There were plenty of empty buildings these days, whistling hollowly whenever the wind blew.

This new job turned a knot in his gut. How could Ms Pointer possibly be important to them? Why did they need her out of the way? He wondered if they were just playing with him for their own amusement. He really didn't want to hurt anyone – he especially didn't want to hurt women – but it seemed they took a particular glee in making him do the things he least wanted to.

The Parliament of Fowls had revealed themselves to him five years ago, after he'd fallen sick (after the world had fallen sick once the flu had jumped from birds to humans). He'd been bedridden with a kind of encephalitis and they'd come to him in his fugues with the sound of wings and birdsong. During his long convalescence they'd sent him a wren. It would sit on his windowsill or bedpost and would eventually hop onto his hand whenever he was alone. He took it as a sign. A sign that he was going to get better, that he had a guardian. The first seven words the Wren ever spoke to him were not shocking, but worked as a balm to his restless, sickening soul. As the world was dying and he was recovering it told him: "There is nothing to be concerned about."

After that the Wren asked him to do things. Small things at first: curse the name of God; steal something inconsequential; break a window; set a fire. Later, they revealed themselves and he came to understand what they truly were. He understood that it was not just his little companion, but all birds. Every single bird on the planet was not what they seemed. They were all part of the Parliament and they had plans which had been cast in the fire aeons ago, made firm by hammer and anvil.

In the last five years they had told him to kill two people. Ms Pointer would be the third.

If he could just find his way to the sea he might have the courage to swim out until the water took him, but these damned cobbled streets kept turning in upon themselves.

He rounded a corner to find his path blocked by a mob of crows. They surrounded a dead cat which had been mauled or hit by something, and not recently. They patrolled on stiff legs, croaking throatily, and poked at its gizzards. Beyond them he thought he spied a route to the sea, but he turned and went back the way he'd come, worried that they may have heard his thoughts.

Birds lined his route now. Gulls hovered overhead like drones while starlings and sparrows sat on gutters and fences, silently marking the turns he must take and the streets to follow to fall back in line. That's when he saw them, about five miles away over the cliffs; hundreds, no thousands of birds circling lazily on some slow column of heat. It was no murmuration, but a widening gyre of all kinds of species gathering for the work to be done. This was a delegation from the Parliament itself, and Mr Barker went cold as he watched more dots join the lazy whirlwind of feathers.

*

He sat in his room for the rest of the day, expecting the Seagull to arrive at any moment with encouragement, threats, or a mixture of the two to secure completion of the job ahead. The oily bird didn't come, though. In fact, for the past couple of hours he hadn't noticed any fluttering or chirrups outside the window.

He popped his head outside, and in the reddening light of evening he saw that the vortex of feathered bodies out over the cliffs had grown. Near him, though, there was no sign of any avian spies. Perhaps they had all joined the throng and no one was here to keep an eye on the errand boy. If he was ever going to run it had to be now, at the height of their bacchanal.

He set off cross country in a succession of fits and starts over unploughed fields, holing up in ditches and thickets between each wheezing sprint. He couldn't run forever; eventually one of them would spot him, perched on a branch, hidden in a hedgerow, or racing high through the air to join the infernal gathering at the coast. If he were far enough away when they caught him, though, she might stand a chance.

He was ten miles away when he saw the figure in the field. It was just a distant silhouette standing with arms wide in welcome. Mr Barker rubbed stinging sweat from his eyes with a shirtsleeve and without a thought of keeping under cover he streaked across the fields towards it as if he were running towards his salvation.

At each moment he expected to hear angry wings and feel the pointed grip of talons in his shoulders or the jagged tear of beaks at his neck. His thighs and calf muscles burned as he pushed forwards over rough soil and stone, sweat mingling with tears now, until he collapsed at the trouser cuffs of the scarecrow, the makeshift crucifixion which had caught his eye. They would not dare approach this ragged reminder of the torture done to their enemy. He could make a stand here and give Ms Pointer a chance to flee.

Fifteen minutes later the first bird dropped out of the sky.

A magpie landed at a distance and cawed a rasping call to arms. As dusk fell, other birds began to join it. By the time the quarter moon was on the rise there were hundreds of things shuffling, clucking and crowing around him in the gathering darkness.

"You can't stay there forever," one said in a voice like tar.

"Running was stupid," said another, and the feathered throng shifted in their loose circle, a stalking murder. They whispered in his head too, of all the things he was ashamed of.

"Do you need reminding of what we really are?" a third voice jibed, and he shook his head ferociously.

In the darkness, beneath the stars, they showed him, and he was too terrified even to scream.

*

"You cheating, cowardly fuck." The Seagull's voice sounded like sandpaper.

It was deep into the night by the time Mr Barker returned, broken, to his darkened room. He reached for the light switch.

"Leave it!" the order froze him.

This was where he would be killed, he was sure of it.

"Bring me a cigarette," the bird said.

Mr Barker pulled out the packet as if he were operating robotic arms. When he struck a match he saw the bird perched on the end of his bed, bathed briefly in the sulphur flare. Its face was mangled.

"My punishment," was all it said once the room was back in darkness. Mr Barker approached gingerly and slid the filter into the creature's beak, then retreated until it was just an orange dot in the shadows. The bird puffed silently for a minute, then in a voice dragged from the pit it drawled: "Now go and kill that bitch."

*

The silence outside Ms Pointer's room screamed "Murder!" as he listened to her heavy breathing through the door. As did the creaking of her hinges and the rub of his stocking feet as he incrementally pushed the door inwards and stole inside.

At her bedside he mouthed "I'm sorry" over and over. Her curtains were open and her skin was smooth in a milky shaft of moonlight. Her blonde hair almost white. He thought her eyes fluttered and he was suddenly afraid that she would open them and see him. He was afraid of the shame he would feel if she saw him standing there. Then he was yanking the pillow out from beneath her head and pushing it into her face before she could scream. She bucked and writhed and he had to lean awkwardly over her body, trying to pin her down with his hip as she scratched and beat at his arms and face. It took longer than he'd anticipated and he was sweating by the time she was limp and gone.

Once his breathing was back under control he pulled a candle from his jacket pocket and lit it with a match. He dripped a pool of wax onto the nightstand and set the candle in place there so he could finish his work. The amber glow banished the soft phosphorescence of the moon. When he lifted the pillow she looked old again.

He froze, terrified by Mrs Tavistock's twisted, grey face. The wrong one. The moonlight had made her look young again and he'd killed the wrong one. Just outside the closed door the Seagull was waiting impatiently. He looked down at her slack expression and tried to pull her skin smooth, make her seem somehow young again, like Ms Pointer. He thought of the bird's rage once it discovered his mistake and he thought of Ms Pointer sleeping innocently in some other room in this large building.

Then came a moment of clarity: she could still live.

He scoured the room: a chair; a small bookcase; a cabinet and dresser. A brass candlestick holder with a thick base sat on the dresser. He brought it to the bedside, tested its weight, then brought it down on Mrs Tavistock's face. The crack of teeth; the breaking of her nose; her eye sockets; he didn't stop until she was unrecognisable. Then he finally saw her face as it would become, not as it had once been.

"You took your sweet time," the bird said as Mr Barker leaned, breathless, against the door jamb. "Ready to finish this?" it croaked through the mess of its face. He nodded, stepped aside, and the bird waddled in. There was one more thing to do.

*

The next morning Ms Pointer sat awkward and alone for breakfast.

The strange young man with hungry eyes did not descend and Mrs Tavistock did not emerge from the kitchen with a choice of canned goods. The wind-up radio was silent.

Eventually, she went searching for the other occupants of the house.

She found Mrs Tavistock in her bed with her face caved in. There was a bloody candlestick holder on the floor beside her, jammy with matted grey hair and pieces of scalp. A seagull was laid out across her chest, its wings splayed and neck broken. Its face was also mangled.

Even after all these years her first thought was to call the police, even though there were no phones anymore and no real police to speak of. After some time she gathered herself enough to pack and leave. She made a trip to the kitchen and retrieved as many cans of food as she could carry.

She could have stayed, she supposed, for a time at least. She wasn't squeamish anymore, not like she'd been before things had turned sour. The idea of staying in this place with a body didn't really bother her. What made her want to flee, though – what made her understand in her very blood that she should leave this place – was the memory which came unbidden the moment she saw the body – the memory of being woken the night before by a cacophony of birdsong.

ESAU AND EMIL

Of all the stories I collected in my travels through the High Country – those mountain forest regions thick with tales of vampires, revenants, and spirits – it is the account of the brothers Esau and Emil which has remained in my thoughts these many years. Perhaps it is because I was shown their graves, or perhaps because of my own brother.

I saw fit to omit the account from my collected works for reasons I will not now broach. I recount it here because my evenings are growing long, and my night will soon fall.

This, then, is the tale as it was told to me, by the wall of a crumbling church grounds.

*

They were autumn babies, and twins, born late to a couple who had long ago given up hoping for children; one the reflection of the other, born no more than one hour apart, and the elder was named Esau and the younger Emil. Such fair-haired and bright-eyed boys they were that their mother would often say they were angels, provided by the Good

Lord to make amends for a long injustice. And truth be told there were those in the town who did not think it too profane to attribute a little of the divine blessing to their arrival. Nor, as the years passed and the small boys could be found dashing about the streets or laughing among the trees, were any of them minded to recant that notion.

True to say that the children provided their mother and father with a second summer towards the end of their lives. But all things turn, and the boys were barely young men before their father died and their mother followed not two years later. After that time some said it became a little easier to mark out which brother was which, for while Emil remained outgoing and with a quick smile, Esau became quieter and more thoughtful. And with each year that passed, although still identical to the eye, the differences beneath their skin became marked. Their parents had loved them the same and had portioned out all care and attention in equal measure between the two boys, but at some point, a worm had burrowed its way into Esau's heart. There it sat and there it grew fat on a thousand imagined slights and grievances.

Now it fell out that sometime after this a travelling group made its way to the town. They set up camp on the outskirts and came within to seek work and to entertain for whatever food or coin they could earn. Among that troupe was a young lady called Sabine. She danced in the square and sang in the inns, turning many an eye and palming plenty a penny. The small children would trip over their feet chasing after her in the streets and the older lads would trip over their tongues trying to impress her in the taverns, for she was a wild and dark beauty, so very different to the girls of the town.

It was one raucous evening in a tavern where she first met Emil, and one solitary afternoon in the forest where she first met Esau. And if she was taken with both men in isolation, she was fascinated by the two when she saw them side by side, so alike and yet so different. She would stroll and converse with Esau by day and sing and dance with Emil in the evening. And soon, without any malice or bad intent, she fell in love with them both, and they in turn both fell in love with her.

In this way those three saw out spring and welcomed summer, but all things turn and soon her travelling family were making plans to move on. It fell that on the feast of St Vitus both brothers in their own way asked Sabine to marry them. She wept for joy at the thought of each earnest proposal, and she wept in sorrow at the hurt she must deal one of the brothers. She consulted the stars, and she consulted the cards. She consulted her elders, and she consulted her heart. Finally, she asked to meet both brothers in the town square two days before her troupe was due to depart. When the three gathered she kissed each brother upon the cheek, calling one "my solemn darling Esau" and the other "my bright darling Emil." She told them that she could no more choose between them than she could decide to live without either the sun or the moon. Instead, she would set a challenge.

"My people will leave in two days' time, and I will leave with them," she said. "However, we will return one year and one day from now. Whoever can provide me with the largest heart before I leave shall have my hand upon my return."

At this Esau travelled throughout the region and bought the largest ox he could find for slaughter. He invited everyone from the town to a large feast, with stew, steak, and blood sausage made from every part of the animal. And to Sabine he offered the heart, as big as her head, served on a silver dish and stuffed with the wild mushroom, spinach, garlic, and onion he had picked from the surrounding land.

"Filled to bursting," he said as he presented her with the prize, "as my heart is for you." And the townsfolk who had gathered for the feast fell to cheering and applause for surely this was the largest heart of which one could conceive.

After the feast Emil came forward with a small wicker basket which he presented to Sabine. The onlookers felt sympathy for him, for he had surely failed the challenge. Yet when the basket was opened a murmur of appreciation passed through the crowd.

"Perhaps," he said, "there is some small amount of offal left over from my brother's feast, for my prize needs feeding." Inside the basket wriggled a tiny puppy, barely weaned. "He is already full of love, nothing but heart, but each day you are away from me his love for you will grow and each day his heart will become larger. I have never known a larger heart than that of a faithful dog." The gathered townsfolk fell to cheering, and it was in this way that Emil won the challenge and won Sabine's hand.

On the day she was to leave Sabine expressed her sorrows to Esau and he accepted them graciously. Emil offered condolences to his brother and Esau gave him his hearty congratulations. In his heart, however, that worm of jealousy began to turn and gnaw. For a year and a day Esau fixed a smile to his face while his insides sickened, and his thoughts darkened. He walked alone deep into the forest where he carved curses onto trees. He fashioned a doll of Emil and filled it with pins. He bought a dog which he called Emil and privately scolded it and lashed it until one day it ran away (or so he told anyone who enquired after it's sudden absence).

With each passing day the worm within him grew fatter, reaching down to twist in his guts and coiling up to lay black eggs in his mind. Yet come the day of Sabine's return and the afternoon of her wedding to his brother, Esau's smile was the widest and his praise for Emil the heartiest it had ever been.

After the ceremony, the celebration spilled out into the town square, and when the sky began to redden Esau slipped away from the throng and stole into the cool dark of the forest. He ranged there, cursing and shouting, thrashing the foliage with arms and legs. He loped deeper into the forest than he had ever roamed before, crying and wailing, until his limbs were heavy and his head was light.

By the time he slowed and stopped the moon was full and high and Esau looked up at it as if it were the face of his own mother. He felt sick and knotted, feverish and cold, and when he brought his hands up to his tear-streaked face they were rough to the touch and his face felt stubbly and coarse.

His head swam and he sank to his hands and knees amongst the ferns, neck stretched back to keep the moon in view. He began to sob, then cry, and finally he screamed up to the moon from his very soul. His mouth grew large, and his voice cracked, soaring into a singular, mournful note as Esau released the howl which had been growing inside him for a year and a day.

He ran back to the town faster than he had ever run in his life, and he stole through the streets, more silent than he had ever been in his life, until he reached his brother's house. There he knocked on the door and heard Emil's voice from within ask, "Who is it at this late hour?"

"It is your brother, Esau."

"It is late, brother," Emil replied, "and it is my wedding night. Can you not return tomorrow?"

"But I am leaving tomorrow," Esau said, "and I have one final gift for you on your wedding night." At this Emil unlocked the door and Esau pushed his way in swiftly and killed his brother with a single blow. Then he loped to the bedroom door and knocked again.

"Who knocks?" said Sabine from within.

"It is your husband, Emil. Let me in," Esau replied.

"And who was at the door at this late hour?"

"It was my brother, Esau. He flew into a jealous rage, and I had to kill him." Sabine came to the door and saw the large beast in the hall and the body on the floor.

"Husband of mine," she said, "you look different."

"This is how a husband presents himself to his bride on their wedding night. He shows himself as he truly is. Just as what is beneath the clothes is exposed, so what is worn on the inside is now worn on the outside."

"And there on the floor? Who is that?"

"That is Esau. He loved you still and came here to murder me and claim you for his own, but I have killed him. Look, see for yourself, do you not recognize him?"

Sabine crouched by the body of her husband but did not cry out or weep for she understood that her life was being measured in moments and her next words could bring her end. She reached down to Emil's hand and said, "Look here, the scoundrel has even taken your wedding band for his own." She slipped off the silver ring and clasped it to her breast.

"Come, wife," Esau said gruffly. "It is our wedding night. I have shown you my insides, it is time for you to show me yours."

"But what of your brother's body here? If it is discovered, you will surely be suspected." Esau considered this and then brushed her aside. He opened his brother's chest and ate his heart and lungs and organs in giant gulps of his great mouth. Then he rose and began to lead Sabine into the bedroom.

"But what of your brother's skin and hair?" she said. "If he is recognized you will surely be arrested." Esau considered once more and then returned to his brother's side. He tore at the skin and hair and hands and feet, gobbling them down until there was nothing left but bones. Then he rose again and began to lead Sabine into the bedroom.

"But what of your brother's bones?" she said. "If they are unearthed you will surely be hanged." And for a third time Esau considered. He crunched and cracked the bones and sucked the marrow from them until there was nothing left.

"There, wife," he said as he rose, "now it is time for us to enjoy our wedding night without further delay."

"Yes, husband," Sabine replied, "but you must wear your wedding band. It is only proper." She held out the silver ring and placed it in Esau's rough palm, now big as a dinner plate.

"My finger is too big," he said.

"Then you must put what is now your outside back inside. Then you will be able to wear your ring and we can be joined."

Esau concentrated and began to fold his thick and sickened outsides back in. And as he shrank his belly began to bulge and he began to rock and moan in pain. And the more he folded back into himself the more distended his stomach became, filled as it was with the skin and bones of his brother, until his guts could no longer contain their meal and they ruptured, bloated with innards, and pierced through with shards of bone. What remained of Emil burst out of Esau and both brothers lay dead upon the floor.

*

The old lady who recounted this tale went on to detail Sabine's long life following that terrible night, but I will defer to discretion. Nor will I name the town these events occurred in, for although she is now long dead, that brave young lady and her descendants deserve their privacy. As do the mortal remains of Emil and Esau, one grave still tended in a plot by the cemetery wall, the other laid beside his brother on the far side of that wall, in unhallowed ground, and covered in a thick mess of purple Aconitum, also known as monkshood or wolf's bane.

THE MEMORY OF BONES

When Anna arrived to open her shop there were police cars at the building site opposite. No flashing lights, but there was yellow tape up and the workmen stood outside the cordon in loose, smoking groups.

"Something's happened across from the shop," Anna was on the phone. "The cops are here. Three cars and a van." She was talking to her best friend – her only friend – Daria. She was on edge because Marco had called her last night. She hadn't answered, of course, but she had no idea how he had gotten her new number. They'd been talking about it as she walked to work.

"Maybe he was lurking outside your shop and got hit by a truck," Daria said.

"Don't say things like that," Anna said, "it's not funny. Hang on, I need to put you down and open up." She slipped her phone into a pocket and unlocked the shutter, raising it with a clatter. She jiggled her key in the door and was met with the familiar bloom of incense and scented candles. The shop inside had been trashed. Displays were knocked over and the stock had been flung everywhere. It looked like the aftermath of rage and that was something that Anna was sickeningly familiar with.

She left the shop immediately, shaking by the time she reached the yellow police tape across the street. She waved and caught the eye of one of the policemen, snagging the attention of a nearby group of workmen at the same time. She could hear Daria calling to her, muffled inside her pocket. The policeman ambled over begrudgingly.

"Officer, please," she said, "someone has broken into my shop." He was the other side of the tape, but closer than she felt was necessary. She could smell his armpits. He didn't say anything.

"I arrived to open up just a minute ago and the place has been wrecked. Someone has broken in."

"Has anything been taken?"

"I'm not sure," she said, forcing herself to sound calm and reasonable so as not to be dismissed. "I saw the damage and came straight over here. Please, I don't even know if he's still inside."

The cop exhaled heavily through his nose.

"Hey, help the pretty lady!" one of the nearby workmen called out. The officer unclipped his radio and wandered off a few steps, muttering something into it. The workman who had called out strolled closer and asked her, "What's the problem?" She explained again, waving an arm at her shop, the door hanging open. Daria was calling from her pocket and Anna retrieved the phone.

"Sorry, but I have to go," she said quickly. "There's been a break in. I'm talking to the police. I'll call you later." She hung up.

"You think they're still in there?" The builder asked, rolling a thin cigarette.

"I don't know," Anna shook her head weakly.

"Probably kids. Or junkie scum. You want I should go over there and check? Crack the little shits' heads?"

"I don't…" she was getting flustered; "I think maybe this policeman will go and check for me."

The builder snorted. "Sure, they might as well do something," he said. "They've done nothing but stand around over there since we called them." He gestured disdainfully towards the gaggle of police inside the building site.

"What —" she began to ask, but the officer returned.

"Stand back," he told her as he lifted the tape and ducked underneath it with a grunt. "Stay here," he said, then strolled across the road and into her shop.

"I think you'll be fine now that Sherlock Holmes is on the case," the builder said, jutting a stubbled chin at the officer's departing back. The sound of low chatter reached them from behind the yellow tape.

"Did somebody get hurt back there?" Anna asked.

Her phone buzzed inside her pocket. A text message; probably Daria.

"Sure. A long time ago" the builder replied, lighting his cigarette. "We found some bones. A skeleton." He let out a sigh of acrid smoke. "It looks like it was a small child."

*

There was no intruder inside the shop. There was no evidence of forced entry at the rear, and from Anna's own testimony the place had been locked up tight from the front. The stockroom out back was in a similar state; boxes were torn open and items strewn about the place.

The officer asked her again if she wanted to make a formal statement. He asked in such a way that he may as well have been asking whether she wanted to waste any more of their time.

The smell of his body odour mixed with the incense sticks scattered around was giving her a headache. Maybe she should just let it go. *No, stop that,* she thought to herself. She wanted an incident number and she wanted something on record, especially if things with Marco were starting up again. The cop tutted and said he'd arrange for someone to come by in the next day or two, then he traipsed back across the road to take up his vigil on a spot of muddy ground behind the tape.

Anna spent the morning clearing away the mess. There was no major damage and nothing appeared to have been taken. Once everything was tidied she thought about flipping the sign on the door and opening the shop for the afternoon. That was when she began to cry. It came in big, shoulder-shaking sobs.

*

Daria stayed with her on the phone all the way home.

"Do you think it was him?" she asked.

"I don't know," Anna said. "It happened the same night he called. Can that be a coincidence?"

"Nothing was taken; nothing wrecked?"

"I had to throw out a little stock, but no, just a big mess. Like someone had thrown a tantrum in there."

Autumn hadn't quite turned to winter but the evenings were getting darker. Anna was grateful for her friend's company on the walk home. A weight had settled onto her throughout the day and she was still carrying it with her. She kept her eyes on dark doorways and alleys; she marked people sitting in cars and was hypervigilant of approaching men.

"Did you tell the police about the call?" Daria asked.

"I could barely persuade him to look inside the shop. I don't know. Maybe when I make my statement."

Someone was walking behind her, matching her pace. She held her bunch of keys in her pocket. She gripped them like a weapon, each one poking out from between clenched fingers like claws.

"If it wasn't him, though," she said, "and I send the police to speak to him, that might just be the excuse he needs to show up again." She was speaking a little louder now, making it obvious that she was on the phone. She moved across the pavement so that the person behind could pass on the inside. That way she could run out into the road if the need arose and not be pinned against the wall.

"Anna, are you sure you don't want me to come over? We can have a girls' night."

"Another time, I'm exhausted, I love you though. Thank you for walking me to my door."

The footsteps behind got closer, came alongside, and a squat man in an overcoat passed by without even a sidewards glance at her. Anna slowed and stopped. She watched him move on then doubled back to her apartment building a few doors back.

"Good that nothing was taken, I suppose," Daria said. "Is that you home now? I hear keys."

"Just going inside now. Stay with me up to my door?"

"Of course."

The light was on in the communal hall. Anna passed the mailboxes – no mail for her – and crossed to the stairs. Her running shoes squeaked on the tiled floor and echoed around the hollow space. The building was old. The stairs rose around a wrought iron lift which rattled up and down like a birdcage. She never used the lift. Three flights up and she was at the door to her apartment, the corridor empty.

"Do you want me to talk to him?"

"Oh, Daria, no. Please don't stir things up. I won't answer and he'll stop calling. It's been almost a year since I last heard from him. He'll get bored and stop. Is that Piccolo I can hear?"

"Yes, the little monster! It's getting to that time when the hairy master demands to go out." Anna laughed at the whines and whimpers she could hear and pictured the pampered little dog pawing at her friend's lap.

"I'm almost in. Thank his Lordship for his patience will you?"

"I will pass your thanks along."

Anna used the key to her flat. She'd been there eight months already but still thought of it as her new flat. Her place; her key. There had been a spare but she'd dropped it down a drain. She wanted to know that the key she held in her hand was the only copy. With another quick glance up and down the corridor she turned the key, slid inside, closed the door and twisted the deadlock with practised speed.

"I'm home," she said with a sigh, turning on the lights, dropping her handbag in the hall and kicking off her shoes. "Thank you, D."

While they were wrapping up the conversation Anna made a swift tour of the apartment, checking each room. She hung up then shrugged off her coat, fetched a glass from the cupboard and the opened bottle of Frascati from the fridge. She carried them both to the bathroom where she turned the hot tap on until it became a steaming jet.

*

Anna woke slowly from a dream of something around her throat.

She struggled against bedclothes which had twisted uncomfortably tight around her. There was a weight on her chest and the sound of little hot breaths which dissolved as she roused. She checked the clock. It was early, but light would soon be bleeding into the sky. There would be no more sleep.

At the shop that day there was an intermittent but steady trickle of browsers and buyers. In the lulls Anna leant on the counter and gazed out across the road. The police tape was still up and now there was a small tent on the muddy ground. There were no workmen on site. For the first time since the previous morning she thought about the little bones which had been found there.

Days passed and the tape came down and construction began again in earnest. Anna would find herself watching the activity there. In quiet moments she thought of the small, sad discovery they'd made while digging foundations.

A female officer visited the shop five days after the break in and took her statement. Anna clumsily tried to ask about the skeleton, feeling foolish, worried that she sounded ghoulish. The officer couldn't tell her anything.

That evening she returned to her apartment and her TV remote control was on the floor in the middle of the living room. It caught her attention instantly. Could she have knocked it onto the floor herself in a hurry to get out this morning? That seemed unlikely. It was quite a way from the sofa where it normally sat. Nothing else appeared to be disturbed, though. Her apartment wasn't very large and from where she stood she could see into part of her bedroom through the open door and across the living space into the open plan kitchen. The bathroom and small closet room were round a corner and out of sight.

She stood still; held her breath; listened.

There was nothing.

The thought that someone had been here while she was out made her go cold. She could leave right now and call the police from the communal hall. And if they arrived and the apartment was empty with nothing to show but a remote control on the floor? She'd fought so hard to be believed before. To be believed over him. She'd lost friends over it. She knew exactly what they'd say about this. They'd say: "If she's imagining intruders now how can we believe what she said in the past?" She didn't know what to do. *She didn't know what to do.*

A dog barked outside on the street.

Someone walked across the flat above her, light thudding footsteps on her ceiling.

Then, from the bathroom, came a hideous, wailing cry. It rose in pitch, bouncing off the tiled walls. Pain, frustration, rage. It didn't stop. Anna fled.

*

"Has anyone in your building got a baby?" Daria asked. Piccolo the rat-dog was ferreting around Anna's apartment, running in and out of rooms, nose to the floor, sniffing like a pig after truffles.

Following Anna's panicked phone call Daria had insisted on coming straight over; she was spending the night and there was nothing Anna could say to stop her. Anna had waited outside the building until Daria rounded the corner, carrying a bag of clothes and wine, with Piccolo skittering along the pavement beside her. They'd ascended together and searched the apartment. Nothing in the bathroom had been disturbed and nothing was out of place anywhere else, just the remote control in the middle of the floor as Anna had said. Now they were both on the sofa; Anna was wrapped in a blanket and Daria had opened a second bottle of wine.

"Sorry?" Anna said. She sounded distant but no longer as jittery as when her friend had first arrived.

"Has anyone got a baby in the building?" Daria repeated. "I'm just wondering if the sound of some screaming brat might have travelled up the pipes or through the ducts or something."

"It came from my bathroom," Anna said flatly and Daria let the subject lie.

They ordered takeaway. After they'd eaten Daria offered Anna half a Valium, which she declined. Anna told her about the bones which had been found on the building site. As tiredness took hold she talked about the small skeleton and Marco and began to jumble them up.

"He nearly broke my arm, you know?" she said dreamily. "He twisted it so hard behind my back. I think he was trying to break it."

"You've told me before," Daria said quietly.

"Did you know that bones hold a memory of breaks and fractures? They heal back stronger."

There was no guest bedroom so Daria made herself a makeshift bed on the sofa.

"I'll stand guard over you out here and the little monster can stand guard over the both of us," she said. "No ex-boyfriends or ghostly babies tonight." Anna smiled wanly and tried to insist once again that Daria take the bed, but she was losing the fight to stay awake.

Daria led her to the bedroom and tucked her in as if she were a child, and then she finished the wine on the sofa before falling asleep herself. She was worried about her friend, not for the first time. As her thoughts began to drift she wondered if she'd be woken in the night by flying remote controls or strange bawling noises. Nothing disturbed her though.

The next morning Anna blearily complained that Piccolo had kept her up "with his snuffling and pattering about." Daria didn't protest, but she knew that her dog had been with her all night, in the crook of her knees on the sofa.

*

The weight across Anna's shoulders never seemed to leave her. She slept badly.

Daria checked in from time to time, a text or a call, but anytime she suggested meeting up Anna demurred. She didn't want to see the look in her friend's eyes, a mixture of worry and uncertainty that she'd seen too many times before.

One afternoon a trio of young girls in the local school uniform entered the shop sheepishly. They looked at the candles and crystals before drifting across to the books, whispering amongst themselves. Anna had been gazing out at the building site where they were sinking concrete into the ground but now she moved round the counter towards them.

"Is there anything in particular you girls are looking for?" she asked. She didn't like to think it, but shoplifting was a problem. There was an embarrassed hush from the girls before one of them said, "Carina wants a book of spells."

"*Love* spells," the other friend added, and those two sniggered whilst the third, presumably Carina, blushed deeply.

"You can't make someone love you," Anna snapped. She'd been blunter than she'd intended, and added in a softer voice, "It's not right to make someone do something against their will. That's not love. But if you're interested in –" something caught her eye through the window. "Excuse me for a moment," she said and walked out of the shop.

She thought she'd seen someone across the road, that builder who had spoken to her the morning of the break in. She wanted to ask him about the bones. She walked out into the road, scanning the site for him, but she had lost him among all the other men. She stood in the middle of the road for a few seconds, uncertain, then turned and went back into the shop. The girls had gone. They hadn't taken anything.

The evenings were darker now. All the way home Anna thought she was being followed and a band of fear tightened around her throat. At her door she felt a different tug of unease at the thought of entering her apartment. The space didn't quite feel like hers anymore. She entered tentatively and made the rounds, room to room, almost expecting a noise or signs of disturbance. Everything seemed normal, but the weight which clung to her persisted.

Later that evening she ran a bath and sat on the edge of the tub as the room filled with steam. The sound of churning water seemed to get louder as growing condensation revealed smudges materialising over all the tiles and across the mirror. They were everywhere. They were tiny handprints.

*

Daria tried to get hold of Anna throughout the next day without joy. She stopped by Anna's shop but it was dark and shut up tight. That evening she went to Anna's apartment and found the door open. Anna wasn't there.

*

The wind whipped through the scaffolding and goaded the plastic sheets into uneasy, crackling life. They bulged and flapped against breeze blocks and concrete.

Anna was breathing hard in the darkness. Getting onto the building site had been relatively easy. The space at night felt strange. She knew that her shop was just across the road, beyond the half-built new walls, but she felt weirdly cocooned here from the world outside. She could see the stars overhead in a way the lights of the city didn't normally allow.

Her phone was vibrating in her pocket and she pulled it out, a little surprised to see the number of missed calls and text notifications on screen alongside Daria's incoming call. The light from the screen ruined her night vision. She answered but found herself blinking away throbbing red and orange after images against the dark.

"Anna, thank God, are you alright? I've been trying to get hold of you all day."

"I'm fine. I've been following the crying."

"Crying? Where are you, I'll come and get you."

"The baby; the child. I think I understand."

"What baby?"

"The baby bones. The baby bones I told you about."

"Oh my God, you're not still obsessing over that are you? Don't you read the local paper? They were monkey bones, Anna."

Another gust of chill wind set the heavy plastic sheets popping and shifting.

"What? No."

"It was in the paper. Someone from the university identified and aged them. Some poor thing kept as a pet, probably by some medieval merchant. Its bones were broken from mistreatment, its teeth were filed down and its back deformed from being kept chained by its neck. I don't know how anyone could do that to a poor little creature."

"A monkey?"

"Anna, is that what's been sending you into a spiral this past fortnight? I've been worried sick about you. I felt guilty. I thought it was about Marco. He visited me a few weeks ago; I should have told you." Anna was blindsided. She rubbed her eyes and suddenly felt very exposed.

"I don't understand." There was a big sigh on the other end of the phone.

"I wanted to tell you face to face," Daria said. "He stopped by my work and persuaded me to talk with him at a nearby café when I took my lunch break. Insisted. He told me about his detox programme and his sponsors. He said that part of his recovery involved making apologies to people he'd hurt in the past. He wanted to reach out to you. I thought it might help you put those things in the past too, so... so I gave him your number."

"Daria, no!"

"I thought it would help you. Where are you? Let me come and get you."

Anna made a strangled, angry noise and sat flat on the floor with her legs bent beneath her. She could still hear Daria's voice and smashed the phone against the ground until the light was dead.

Her best friend. How could she?

And no child? Instead an animal, torn from its mother's arms; chained; beaten its whole short life as a trophy, a status symbol.

Another noise escaped her throat, a high keening noise she didn't realise was coming from her. The plastic was flapping violently now. Her eyes were getting accustomed to the dark again in time to see a shape move out of the shadows and move towards her. She looked up at Marco as he approached. Her mouth bobbed open but she couldn't form any words.

"Anna," he said gently.

He crouched down in front of her, squatting on the balls of his feet.

"I've been trying to reach you. I almost stopped you in the street a dozen times. I've been doing a lot of thinking and there are some things I want to say to you." He swallowed. "And you haven't made it easy. You're still a self-involved, selfish little cunt, aren't you?" He made a grab for her hair and she jerked backwards, skidding away on her backside.

There was a scream – was it her screaming? – the same rising wail she'd heard from her bathroom.

Marco was standing now and she scrabbled away on all fours. It seemed as if another small, dark shape moved quickly between them, and then Marco was knocked to the ground, flailing. There was a red moment of angry teeth and nails, throat and face. Marco's high-pitched shriek became wet, bubbled, and then was cut short.

Anna stumbled out of the building site. She walked directly home through midnight streets without a backwards glance. The weight was still with her, across her back and around her neck like a small, strong arm. It no longer felt like fear, though. It felt like armour.

Once home she showered and slept.

There would be police cars opposite her shop again in the morning.

ORPHEUS DESCENDS

Callum barely noticed the ocean swell and the frigid bite of the wind as he stood on deck beneath the northern lights. Seeing those shimmering bands of green and gold as they snaked across the night sky tickled something devout at his core – a place within where he was still the small boy who believed the nuns when they told him that Jesus was always watching him. He'd abandoned his faith long ago, but the aurorae stirred the same sickly mix of excitement and fear he used to get as a child whenever he'd studied the wounds of Christ.

He never thought he'd climb into a submersible again following the accident, but after two years on land an email came seeking expert advice. That had led to more emails, some phone conversations, then a couple of meetings and meals which he later realised had probably been interviews. He'd been headhunted without realising it, and when the offer finally came it had truly been too good to pass up.

He'd worked with universities before, with maritime and oceanographic institutes, and had spent three years working for the BBC on Blue Planet II, but this was unlike any previous job. Now he was the personal submersible pilot for an extremely rich businessman, but this was not some one-percenter trying out a new toy with a series of Caribbean dips. In the last eight months they'd dived in the Gulf of Mexico, in the Tyrrhenian and Aegean Seas in the Mediterranean, the Black Sea and the Baltic Sea. They'd just left the forbidding darkness of the North Sea and now their ship, *The Lyre*, was travelling further north, into the Arctic Circle.

The purpose of the expedition and the dives was a mystery to Callum. The tech on board *The Lyre* was impressive but they took none of it with them beneath the surface; no monitors or recording equipment. His boss wasn't interested in learning to pilot himself, either. He just seemed content to dive and rove beneath the waves and observe.

Callum's new boss was a man called Carter Ealing Marshall. They met long after the background checks had been completed and the contracts signed. Marshall was a tech billionaire, and Callum thought that he was probably having the kind of late-life breakdown that only the ultra-rich could afford. The pay was ridiculous, though, and Marshall's expectations were clearly defined and reasonable, so after a while it became easy to push any questions to one side and do the job. And so, for eight months they had sailed a good chunk of the globe and dove at the whim of Carter Ealing Marshall. They were due to dive again in the morning and Callum needed a decent night's sleep, so he took himself below decks to his berth before the growing chill in the air began to gnaw in earnest.

The next morning, *The Lyre* rocked among stark ice floes on the cut topaz water of the Arctic Ocean. Callum sat inside the snug acrylic sphere of *Orpheus*, running a final check on the two-person mini-sub. The overhead hatch was open and cold, briny air stung his cheeks like a slap to the face.

Carter Ealing Marshall was on the aft deck, having what looked like a very intense discussion with his personal assistant, but Callum couldn't hear what was being said. Deckhands were clambering over the vehicle, attaching it to the bulky crane which would hoist *Orpheus* from the back of the ship into the freezing waters. The clanking noise they made drowned out everything else, but it was clear from the way Marshall was now stabbing the air with his finger that any discussion had devolved into a series of staccato instructions.

Callum girded himself. If Marshall was in a tetchy mood then the next few hours would not be fun. The billionaire pulled off his thick puffer jacket, passed it to his assistant, and visibly caught his breath at the whip of the wind. He had a California perma-tan and the gauntness some older fitness freaks attain which put Callum in mind of Roy Scheider or Buzz Aldrin. He'd only ever seen the billionaire ingesting repulsive looking green or brown smoothies, handed to him by his assistant. The old man was taking this life-prolonging health kick a little too far, Callum thought. He couldn't be sure, bundled up as everyone was in these latitudes, but he thought that Marshall might have even lost a few pounds since they'd started this expedition.

Marshall crossed the deck and clambered onto *Orpheus*. His feet and legs slipped past Callum's face as he dropped into the empty right-hand seat. The temperature controls inside their seven-inch-thick acrylic bubble would keep them warm, but both men still wore fleeces against the chill of the deep. With the boss aboard everything moved quickly. *Orpheus* was plucked from the deck and placed, bobbing, onto the ocean behind the ship. Deckhands uncoupled them from the crane and hopped back on board *The Lyre*. Then, at the "go thrusters" signal, Callum manoeuvred them away from the ship and out into the wide, deep ocean.

Clear blue water lapped around their main ballast tanks, the two yellow pontoons either side of them. Waves rocked them, like riding a cow. Through the bottom of the bubble they got their first glimpse of the cold waters beneath dropping down beyond light.

"What do you say?" Marshall asked, "shall we see what's down there?"

"Yes, sir," Callum said, then flipped on the radio and spoke into his headset. "Topside, topside, this is *Orpheus*."

"Topside reads you *Orpheus*, go ahead," crackled the response from *The Lyre*. The ship seemed much smaller now there was open water between them.

"My hatch is secure; life support is running. Looking for permission to open vents."

"Copy: hatch secure; life support systems running. You're clear to vent."

"Roger that, opening vents now."

This was the moment. Every time.

Since taking this job and returning to the sea, this was the moment Callum had to steel himself against. With each roll and pitch of the sub he felt the water beneath them eager to suck them down.

He cleared his mind, banished irrational thoughts, and released air from their main ballast tanks in a loud hiss. The seawater around them churned into a broiling froth and the hungry waterline climbed like grasping hands up the sides of their bubble. He pushed forwards on the joystick and gently angled them down, using the thrusters to drive them deeper. Once the waves met above them he levelled off. They were calmer now, no longer buffeted by the noise and motion of the surface, and he stilled any remaining unquiet thoughts.

They hung for a while in this new world. Above them the vibrant surface sparkled, shining with scattered light. The electric blue of the upper ocean stretched out around them, giving the illusion that they could see for miles. Then, by degrees, everything dropped out of sight into absolute darkness below.

"Where would you like to go first, sir?" Callum asked.

Marshall pulled a sharp breath in through his nose and held it. He half closed his eyes and looked for all the world as if he were analysing scents he'd caught on a breeze. He grasped something in his hand, a totem or trinket Callum assumed, some New Age hippy thing he brought on all his dives.

"Take us under the ice," Marshall said with a wave. Callum took them deeper and the dive began in earnest.

For the next ninety minutes they glided in silence through fields of marine snow, constellations of tiny, hovering invertebrate life, following the tides of Carter Ealing Marshall's whim. They saw the silver flash of fish and the occasional harp seal chasing down a meal. Callum focused on the instruments, but more fanciful thoughts began to chime in the back of his mind.

Two beluga whales rose out of the shadows, ghostly white with friendly, human-looking, foetal faces. The upturn of their mouths made it seem as if they were regarding the vessel with bemused curiosity. Their visit was fleeting, though, and they soon followed the fish back down into the darkness.

Sailing in silence underneath these huge capstones of ice set something humming in Callum like a plucked string. The ceiling of thick, blue-white sheets spoke to him of frozen cathedrals above their heads. The shafts of turquoise light they swept through seemed to be the upper architecture of measureless, vaulted crypts beneath. Nature was an ancient church.

The first shark came about twenty minutes later. The grey, languorous beast slowly ribboned its way towards them out of the distant murk. It was at least twenty feet long, certainly larger than their craft. Its body was rounded like a fat cigar and its hide was marbled grey and white, mottled like decaying flesh. It moved without hurry, its long tail working the frigid waters like a colonial punkah fan, silently propelling it's one tonne bulk forwards.

"A Greenland shark," Marshall said as the huge fish swam closer.

It's eyes – set back from a pitted, stubby nose – were nothing but flat, pearled cataracts. It was blind and had stringy, white parasites hanging from each eyeball, burrowing into the tissue there. The appearance of the shark buoyed the old man.

"No one knows how long they live," he said, as it passed about six feet from the vehicle. "Certainly two-hundred years; maybe twice that." To Callum it looked like a dead thing which had been stirred into motion as it turned, rolled away from the sub, and began a languid, unhurried dive. "This creature may have been born as the *Mayflower* left Plymouth for the New World," Marshall said as it dropped out of sight. They watched as it was swallowed by the darkness below, and for a moment Callum thought that he saw a pair of faint red lights down there in the depths. "They are the memory of the sea," Marshall said. "We'll dive here."

Callum released more air from the ballast tanks and they dropped into the mesopelagic or "twilight" zone, leaving the reach of the sun. The descent was smooth and it didn't feel as if they were sinking, instead it seemed as if the glowing light around them was steadily dimming. They dropped into perpetual night and the muted cockpit lights grew more vivid as everything outside became dark. Callum kept a keen eye on his gauges, bringing them to a depth of 450 metres before levelling off. He reached to turn on the exterior spotlights.

"Leave them for a while, will you?" Marshall said. "Let's just sit."

The glow from the instrument panel seemed to smooth out the old man's face and make him young again. They sat in silence for three or four minutes, everything black outside their tiny bottle of topside light.

"I've been looking back over your résumé, Callum," Marshall said. "You ever think that you're a touch too qualified to be chauffeuring some old, rich guy around Neptune's back yard?" This was unexpectedly blunt.

"I...er...I," Callum said in a very British way.

"Why do you think I picked you?"

"Well," Callum said, "these aren't joyrides, sir; that's clear. I've got extensive experience. And while I can't pretend to know what these dives are for, I think that —"

"I'm not interested in what you think," Marshall said, "I want to know what you *feel*. What do you feel when you're down here?"

That plucked the string at Callum's core again, set it thrumming.

Something struck *Orpheus*, rocking it. Callum swore and flicked on the spotlights. The black water turned pearly white and lit the blind, dead eye of a Greenland shark right by his head. Over Marshall's shoulder a second shark loomed towards them. It rammed the submersible with its stubby nose, lurching them back in the other direction.

"What the hell?" Callum spat as both sharks spun like ballerinas, flicked their large tails, and nudged *Orpheus* again. One went low, the other glided overhead, exposing its round, speckled belly. Callum reached for his joystick just as a third pointed face lunged, dead ahead, slamming the curved plastic. The noise of each strike was loud inside the cockpit. Callum knew that *Orpheus* was incredibly strong, but he wasn't eager to test its integrity against three beasts each larger than a Cadillac.

"Why are they behaving like this?" he asked; "surely it's not our lights?" He glanced at Marshall who had one palm flat against the roof of the bubble. He couldn't tell if the old man was bracing himself or trying to stroke the shark which was now rolling against the top of their vehicle, thumping the hatch. Callum dearly wanted to surface, but first he had to get out from under this monstrous fish. He jammed the joystick forwards and angled them down with *Orpheus'* thrusters. The sounds inside the cockpit became amplified: the hiss of their CO_2 scrubber now sounded like an air leak, and the metallic impacts from outside crunched like a car crash – and for a moment he was back inside a spinning car, leaving the road, tyres squealing like an injured pig, but quickly drowned out by the screams of his passenger.

Orpheus dipped forwards and down like a fairground ride. The sweep of its spotlights arced through a starfield of zooplankton and strange, floating bodies. They found themselves in a bloom of jellyfish and Callum drove the sub down and through it. He glimpsed the flash of a squid in the moving beam, darting away from the light. Then, beyond that, at the very limit of the light's reach, he saw something moving. Something impossibly vast.

"Jesus!" he barked, instinctively yanking the joystick back, jarring them like a dodgem car. He went cold and flicked off the spotlights. He didn't want them to look too bright and inviting to that huge thing. They needed to get back to the surface fast.

"Did you see that?" he asked, lifting them back into the cloud of jellyfish, imagining a gigantic mouth in the deep opening and rising to meet them. Marshall looked ashen and rapt and said something halfway between an exhalation and a moan, a word Callum couldn't make out, but which seemed to be all vowels. It sounded for all the world like a prayer.

"Did you see it?" Callum grabbed the radio headset, expecting teeth as big as men to appear from the black at any moment. Marshall was fumbling with something, that totem of his. Then came an explosion of bubbles all around them.

Callum braced himself, certain they'd been struck again. He yanked on the joystick but couldn't feel any pitch or yaw; the thing was dead in his hands and the thrusters were silent. Something was very wrong. The old man was making a strange noise in the back of his throat. The depth gauge said they were dropping. He realised: the blast of bubbles just now, their main ballast tanks had vented all their remaining air. They were sinking.

"Reach the ship," he said, thrusting the headset at Marshall and flipping on the radio. "Tell them we've had an electrical failure. I'm going to bring us up, but it won't be pretty."

Even with the main ballast tanks flooded *Orpheus* had a variable tank at the rear. He could fill that with compressed air and make them lighter than water again. He engaged it, anticipating the deep hiss, but nothing happened. He tried the switch a couple more times before moving to the override which would let him pump air into the tanks manually.

Marshall was calling *The Lyre* and Callum kept an ear out to ensure that the ship above them was responding before focussing once again on his return to surface protocols. The depth gauge said they were still sinking. Callum kept pumping. It was not possible for the electronic and manual systems to fail in unison, but he had a third option, he could jettison the battery pods and make them lighter that way. The only time he'd ever done that was back in training. No pilot ever expected to have to use that method to get back topside, but he gave a silent prayer of thanks to the team who had designed this craft. He pulled the release and heard a dull clunk beneath them. The depth gauge continued to fall. He pulled the release again and once more there was a clunk. Still falling.

"Come on, come *on!*" he kept yanking the release and the instrumentation told him they were now 830 metres down and falling. Marshall was silent and still, watching him like an owl. "We're in trouble," Callum said, "let me speak to the ship." Marshall slipped the headset off and held it out wordlessly, his eyes never leaving Callum's. Then came a new noise, a low groan of metal. *Orpheus* was not designed to operate much deeper than 1,000 metres. Callum gritted his teeth, afraid to look at the depth gauge. He pulled the battery pod release one more time then tried the variable ballast tank again, moving like an automaton, his eyes becoming glazed. *Orpheus* moaned in complaint once more.

"Mayday, mayday, mayday, this is *Orpheus* do you copy?" all life had drained from his voice. He was covered in a cold sweat and his vision was getting spotty. He thought he might black out, which would be a nice way to avoid what was going to happen next. If they continued to fall then their robust little globe would give in under unimaginable pressure. There was a crackle on the radio, a distant voice, and then a sudden, crunching bang. An instant more would bring the crushing inward rush of freezing black water.

Except that did not happen.

For a few seconds there was only the white noise of the CO_2 scrubber, then another creak as *Orpheus* tilted a little. A judder ran through Callum's legs and buttocks then up his spine. His breath came in stabs and every moment he expected to be pulped inside a tight fist of ocean water. The depth gauge said they were 1,129 metres deep and holding. That crunch made sense to him now, they had hit the seabed and were settling.

Neither man moved. They barely breathed. The lights from the instrument panel seemed to dim, but Callum thought that might be blood leaving his head and blurring his vision. Some structural part of *Orpheus* was under stress and was protesting. The globe they sat in felt suddenly fragile, like a bubble of soapy water waiting to pop. There were other noises, perhaps from outside.

"Topside, topside, do you read me? Mayday, mayday, mayday. This is *Orpheus*, do you read?" Callum's voice was a monotone. He repeated the transmission. Then again, cycling through the words emotionlessly, trying to get to grips with the size of their predicament. They were over one kilometre down, at the very limits of the kind of depth stress their vehicle could withstand. They couldn't ascend. *Orpheus* had a subsea locator; that meant *The Lyre* knew exactly where they were. She would have seen them drop and she would know that they'd bottomed out. "Mayday, Mayday, topside do you read?" They had air; they had life support. The systems had failed catastrophically.

There was no way the people on the surface would leave this super-rich asshole stranded down here, Callum thought. There would be a Board of Directors somewhere, probably even now, moving mountains to bring Marshall up and safeguard company stock prices. There was no other submersible on *The Lyre*, though, and no way anyone on board could scuba down to them this deep and this cold. They were in the God-damned Arctic Ocean. Cold panic began to rise like bile. Don't think like that. Greenland wasn't that far away. This guy had connections, he had influence. Hell, the Navy were probably already on their way.

"Your people," Callum said, and his voice cracked. "I can't reach the ship. They... they need to..." The electronics were shot, but not all of them. That didn't make sense. He should have been able to inflate the ballast tanks manually. The thought that *Orpheus* might have been sabotaged squirted like liquid nitrogen in his mind. If Carter Ealing Marshall was too rich to abandon might that make him, for some, rich enough to kill? "They have a contingency plan, right?"

"My people know what to do," Marshall said. The old man sounded a little spacey. He took a tentative, deep breath, then shifted in his seat, glancing around at the inside of their bubble. In the muted light of the cockpit all they could see was their own curved reflections in a dark mirror.

"Do you think that maybe –" Callum started.

"Do the searchlights still work?" Marshall said, sounding faraway. "I'd like to see where we are."

"Mr Marshall, the… our situation –" Marshall was leaning forwards, reaching for the switch which would light them up like a signal fire. Callum thought of that huge shape he'd seen moving in the deep. He grasped the man's bony wrist and spat "Don't" through gritted teeth. "There's something… I saw something." His thoughts became watery. What had he seen? Something moving just beyond the reach of the spotlights; something large enough to turn his thoughts into a scream from just a glimpse of it. But how could that be? Maybe it had been a shoal of tightly clustered fish turning away from the sudden light and the poor visibility made them look alien. A sperm whale, perhaps? They ventured into Arctic waters. No, what he'd seen had been much larger than that.

"Callum," Marshall freed his hand and placed it firmly on his pilot's shoulder. "Listen to me." The old man dipped his head to meet Callum's eyes and the shadows in the cockpit made his cheeks look bony and his eye sockets hollow. Callum's jittery mind sent him back to his childhood for a few seconds, to the whispered darkness of the confessional and the silhouetted authority of the priest. He met Carter Ealing Marshall's gaze and felt the weight of the church in it.

"Callum listen to me," Marshall repeated. "Every contingency has been planned for; you understand? Even when I'm not on board my orders are carried out. Even if I'm at the bottom of the ocean. They're up there right now following my instructions to the letter." Callum swallowed, nodded, then tried to get his breathing under control. He inhaled deeply then let it out shakily. He didn't catch the thin wisp his breath became, but some part of the back of his mind had already noticed that it was getting colder.

Orpheus creaked again, maybe settling, maybe stirred to sobbing pain by an underwater current or something passing nearby. They sat and waited. Occasionally Callum would try the ballast tanks and the manual overrides, but eventually the gaps between each attempt grew longer. He continued to transmit regular mayday messages until it felt as if he were broadcasting into outer space. Throughout all this Carter Ealing Marshall remained silent and still and the temperature continued to fall. Soon their breath came in plumes and eventually they both sat soundless in the gloom of the cockpit.

"I lost my daughter," Marshall broke a long stretch of silence and then seemed to sink into another. It was some time before he spoke again. "A man in my position must make a lot of sacrifices. We weren't close for many years. I think it was my faith which drove her away. I kept tabs on her; hoped for a reconciliation; then one day she was taken from me." Callum was shivering by now.

He'd pulled the sleeves of his fleece over his hands and was hugging them under his armpits.

"I'm sorry, I didn't know." he said.

"You don't know what it's like to have a child."

"No, I don't have children."

"I know you don't. Not even any running around that you don't know about." Callum turned to him, confused. "My background checks are very thorough," Marshall said before wallowing in another stretch of silence.

"Do you know I read her autopsy report?" he said, eventually. "And then a few weeks after that my consultant told me that I was dying. It focuses the mind. I think it's time we have a look at where we are now." He reached for the spotlights again and this time Callum did not move to stop him.

With a flick the darkness outside withdrew a short distance as a circle of milky white light sprang up around them. The water was thick with sediment stirred up by their rough landing. The lunar-looking seabed stretched away from them for maybe 10 or 12 feet before abruptly ending at the edge of a pitch-black fissure. The fissure was wider than the reach of the lights and fell away to unknowable depths. Callum couldn't take his eyes off that gulf. If they had been a few feet further in that direction they would have continued to drop and would have been mashed inside their imploding vehicle. He set about another round of system checks and radio transmissions. They had been underwater and under the ice for nine hours now.

Over time Callum's thoughts became unmoored. There were periods when he was at the controls, transmitting or trying to get the tanks to fill, and spells when he floated elsewhere, suspended outside time. One time his wandering mind returned to the sound of Carter Ealing Marshall quietly sobbing – or was he praying? – and he wanted to reach across or say something, but he didn't move. Another time it was quiet in the cockpit again and they were surrounded by a silent electrical storm of bioluminescence, and Callum wondered if he had imagined the sobbing. Sometimes he felt drunk, couldn't think straight, and the cold sent his mind retreating once more.

He'd been drifting elsewhere like that when pain brought him back to himself. It felt as if something was chewing his feet off. Marshall was curled up in an awkward ball in the seat next to him, his feet off the floor. Callum slowly realised that his own feet were sitting in a few inches of freezing seawater which had gathered in the footwells. They had gone completely numb and the nerve endings around his ankles were on fire. He pulled them up and hugged his knees as his body shook against the cold.

"How long?" he asked. He had to repeat the question a few times before Marshall turned to face him. "How long until your people get here?" Marshall studied him with those owl eyes again.

"How long did it take before anyone showed up at Lough Erne?" Marshall said through gritted, chattering teeth. "How long before you were able to flag down a car and have someone call for help?" Callum struggled to follow the thread of words; they sounded like nonsense, then comprehension came – of course Marshall would know about the accident.

"I know a lot about the incident," Marshall sounded almost as if he were talking to himself. "I read all the articles; I read the coroner's report; I even listened to your recorded interviews with the police. Oh, don't look shocked," he laughed but it sounded like a bark. "There really is nothing that money can't buy. But there are details missing; things I'd like to know while we have the time. If you don't mind looking back."

Lough Erne in County Fermanagh, Northern Ireland. The accident. An argument in the drizzly gloaming of an autumn evening; driving too fast; that first screech of tyres and the steering wheel wrenching out of his grip as they spun and left the road.

"I don't understand," Callum said.

Faye's scream. The dull crump as they span into the lake and the sudden clench in his chest when that freezing water rushed into the car.

"There's one detail; one thing," Marshall said. "Despite all the records and interviews and official accounts, there's one thing I'd really like to know. I'd be indebted to you if you could answer it for me."

The water had tasted dirty, full of silt. The freezing shock of it had set his pulse fluttering, threatening cardiac arrest as he'd wrangled with his seatbelt and the door handle. Door open; rising with an eruption of bubbles; he'd seen the twin red rear lights of the car falling away below him.

"Tell me," Marshall said, "did you really try and dive back down to get her out? Did you really dive back down three times, like you told the police, to try and pull her free? My Faye? My daughter?" Callum's body became wracked with shivering. The old man's breath hung about his head in a mist. "I read my own daughter's autopsy report. Do you want to know how many fingernails she lost trying to claw her way out of that car?" Callum was sobbing now, and *Orpheus* gave a pained metallic cry as if in sympathy. "When you left that submerged car do you think that any of the air bubbles you rose with were Faye's last scream? Do you think her last thoughts might have been a curse on you? Water remembers, you know."

"When will your people get here?" Callum keened like a toddler. "When will they get here? When will they get here?" From the depths of the fissure there came a low, steady rumble. It wasn't a geological sound. It sounded as if it came from deep in the back of something's throat.

"What's out there?" Callum's voice was small. Marshall was staring at the fissure, his face a mask of rapt awe.

"Have patience," the old man said; "we'll both meet it soon enough, although in different capacities." He looked at Callum with genuine pity. "I'll be going outside soon. There's much that I could try to explain, but how does an angler explain the carp to the mealworm? I've been dipping you into the sea all over the globe and you've finally done your job." Marshall raised a shaking hand, clutching the totem he'd brought on every dive. Not a totem, though, Callum saw now. It was something squat and black and electrical.

"Rigging the sub to fail was easy," Marshall said, then he brought the little device down hard on the control panel, smashing it. His eyes grew wide and he began to sing. It sounded like a hymn, although Callum couldn't understand the words. It didn't matter, though, because in that moment he had lost his mind.

He was screaming. His fingers were scrabbling at the clasps to the hatch above their head. Marshall's singing grew louder. Callum pushed at the hatch with all his strength but the water pressure outside was so great there was no chance of opening it even a fraction. Then his fingers were at the old man's throat. He was making a high, screeching noise as he dug into leathered flesh and pushed his thumbs as deep into the old man's larynx as they could go. The sound of screeching tyres filled his head and he was shouting into Carter Ealing Marshall's slack face. He shouted for a long time.

After that there were only moments of lucidity. One time he was shocked to see a thick smear of blood on the inside of their bubble and his hand throbbed, knuckles swollen and bleeding, probably broken. He must have been hammering at the acrylic for a long time.

Another time he was trying to push Marshall's sagging body away from him with his feet. He wished the old man's eyes were closed but he didn't want to reach out and touch that grey face.

At some point he must have turned out the searchlights, probably so as not to see the old man's body. When he'd died Carter Ealing Marshall had emptied his bowels and Callum was gagging now, struggling to breathe. Pins and needles of cold pricked at every part of his exposed skin and he shook constantly. He wondered if he might summon the courage to touch the old man long enough to pull off his fleece jacket. He wanted to stand up. He wanted to stretch his legs. He wanted to get out of this tiny cell. He screamed for a long time.

The radio crackled.

He couldn't feel his face and didn't realise he'd been biting into his lips until a well of warmth – his own blood – filled his mouth and spilt down his chin. The sputter of transmission came again and he looked around the cockpit groggily, as if he were waking to a strange alarm in an unfamiliar room. He slowly located the origin of the sound and then blinked thoughtlessly a few times at the headset which lay across his controls in front of him. The digital hiss came again and it sounded like a voice. His right hand was a throbbing, swollen claw, so he retrieved the headset with his left and awkwardly hooked it over his head one-handed. His jaw was clamped tight against the cold and he grunted, hoping the microphone would pick it up. Another burst of static hissed in his ear. He grunted again and the static resolved into a faint voice.

"Can you hear me?"

He grunted louder, up into a whine.

"Callum? Can you hear me?" the signal got a little clearer. It was a woman's voice. "Callum, why did you leave me down here? I couldn't get out and it was so cold, so very cold. Why did you leave me?" He began to whine and the note rose until he sounded like a wounded animal, exhausted in a trap. He snatched the headset off and cast it aside. From wherever it fell he could still hear the plaintive question in amongst the digital cracks and pops. That was when he realised that Marshall's body was not in the opposite seat.

The footwells were now completely submerged; the water which filled them was oily black. Callum wondered if perhaps Marshall's body had slumped down and was now underwater, but the footwells were surely too small to conceal him. He scrambled onto his knees and reached down into the water lapping at the opposite seat. It was so cold that it felt as if he'd plunged his arm up to the elbow into boiling oil. He pulled it back with a scream and cradled it against his chest. As brief as his search had been, though, it was enough to confirm that there was no body beneath the stinging ink.

"Callum," the small voice from the headset said, "turn on the lights." He began to cry and wanted to say "No," but he just kept repeating a noise.

"Turn on the lights. Turn on the lights. Turn on the lights."

He reached out with a palsied left arm and did as he was told. The exterior lights conjured an instant pale stage, much clearer of disturbed sediment now. The craggy seabed appeared at a Dutch angle because *Orpheus* had landed askew. A few feet away Cater Ealing Marshall stood on the edge of the precipice. He turned slightly at the sudden illumination and looked back over his shoulder with a sorrowful look on his face. Then he hopped forwards over the rim and dropped away out of sight. Now Callum's lips and tongue managed to form the word "No" and he screamed it again and again, staring at the void out beyond the edge of the fissure.

Strange creatures occasionally passed the vehicle. They looked prehistoric, evolved to survive the crushing depths, and were indifferent to the screaming man inside his strange bauble of light.

Eventually Callum's shredded voice gave out completely, but his raw eyes never left the edge of the fissure and the spot where Carter Ealing Marshall had impossibly leapt. His face and hands felt hot now. So cold that it felt as if his skin was burning. He wanted to peel it off. The headset was crackling again. His breath bloomed in large, fleeting clouds about his head.

At the fissure's edge something was happening. A hand reached up out of the void and gripped the seabed. Callum began shaking violently. A second hand reached up and clawed at the ground, sending up a puff of silt. Those hands now strained and hauled up a head and body behind them, long hair wafting like seaweed around a puffy, blue face. Even before this figure had finally, clumsily, clambered up over the precipice, Callum was gnawing at his own wrists like a crazed rat. The figure got to its knees, then staggered up to its feet, immune to the crushing pressure. A dark current parted the wreaths of hair, and even though her face was swollen with water Callum recognised Faye.

In the time it took her to take just two steps – sediment rising around each footfall – the water inside *Orpheus* had reached something vital. Sparks and sharp smoke filled the cockpit and all the lights cut out. Callum continued to bite at his wrists, desperate to feel the hot gush which would end this, but his frozen mouth couldn't get purchase on the thin skin there.

In absolute darkness spots of light bloomed behind his eyes. Then came the knocking, steady and insistent on the outside of the cockpit. Faye's voice was coming through the radio again, calling his name. The blobs of light danced and merged into two points of throbbing red.

Somewhere in the darkness a vast mouth began to open.

THE SHADES OF MIDWINTER

Granny and I sat by the fire while Ma hovered at the window with her hot chocolate, surveying the darkness outside.

This was our first Christmas since Ollie died and Dad left. We'd driven through the night, far up into the Highlands, to reach Granny before the snow arrived which cut off her village each year. Every room in our house felt empty now, and the journey north felt more like we were running away than travelling to be with family.

Granny lanced more marshmallows and passed them to me to hold over the flames, but my mother's strange vigil kept snagging my attention.

"I don't see anything yet," Ma muttered without turning. I could see her wan reflection in the dark glass. She looked worried. I wanted her to be okay, but nothing would ever be okay again.

"What's she looking for?" I whispered. Granny tutted and shook her head. The lenses of her thick glasses were full of flames.

That morning we'd woken to a muffling blanket of white which seemed to deaden the air of the small valley. We'd gone outside and joined the rest of the villagers who were making snowmen, one for each of the twenty-three men, women and children who lived there. Even Granny. We had to wheel her out but she insisted on patting out a crooked, cold body and head as best she could with her bent, arthritic hands.

"Don't forget your token," she said as she puffed and strained, waving away any offer of help. Ma had explained the tradition on the way up, something she'd done each midwinter as a little girl: you roll something personal into the body of your snowman, near the heart. Everyone in the village did it.

Now Ma kept watch over our effigies while Granny and I sat in the crackling orange circle of heat. Granny put a crooked finger to her lips and let me have a sip of her mulled wine while Ma was distracted. I pulled a face but took another sip when the mug was offered again.

Ma inhaled sharply and I snapped my head around. I was up and at her side before Granny could stop me. There were three shadowy figures on the lawn by our snowmen.

"Who are they?" I asked, but no one answered.

The fire popped.

As I cupped my face to the window I saw that there were more silhouettes standing outside other houses too. Each one was standing beside a snowman.

"Ma, what's going on?"

"I thought I'd imagined it," she murmured to herself, "all those years ago."

"Don't worry, petal," Granny said, "the shades don't bother us if we leave our tokens in our stead."

"You did leave a token didn't you?" Ma asked. Her expression frightened me.

"I thought," I stammered. "I thought Ollie should be here with us. I put his toy truck in my snowman." I didn't understand what was happening.

There was a light, dull knock at the door.

"Don't answer it!" Granny shouted.

A hollow, plaintive cry came from the other side.

"Ollie!" my mother called out and rushed to the door.

"Don't!"

Ma opened the door but her wide smile froze to something rictus as the cold charged in and filled the room.

IN THE SHADOW OF THE TSUNAMI

Morwenna felt it coming. It was their third night in Thailand and Beverley had been trying to pick a fight with her all day. The argument finally broke during a late supper in a small restaurant near Bang Niang Beach. Morwenna, as ever, tried to placate her girlfriend as people from nearby tables began to turn and look, but Beverley was drunk and she was becoming cruel.

"Can you step outside your head for one minute and look around you?" Beverley said. "Pulling that fucking face at the local food." She scrunched her own face up, mocking Morwenna. "We were supposed to leave that small-minded shit at home, not drag all your hang-ups halfway around the world with us."

"Bevvy, I just don't like the look of the squid."

The humidity of the day had given way to a less oppressive, but more personal heat. Morwenna felt the prickles at the nape of her neck and between her shoulder blades. The clattering hiss of woks from the open kitchen was almost constant, like some antiquated steam engine on the verge of collapse. The aroma of fish, spices and exotic cooking rolled over her. She acquiesced for the sake of a peaceful meal and took a mouthful of squid from the end of her girlfriend's outheld fork and tried not to gag as the lump of rubbery flesh sat in her mouth like a second tongue. She swallowed even as her stomach did flips and Beverley fell into a sullen display of stabbing at her food and chewing robotically.

Something in Morwenna's chest rippled, a small sadness.

At the same time, hundreds of miles out to sea, a huge fault line exploded in violent earthquake with the energy of thousands of atomic bombs. The seabed rose by several metres, displacing massive volumes of water and sending out shockwaves in all directions.

After their meal Morwenna persuaded Beverley to walk down to the beach to watch the sunset. They held hands loosely. Bev was quiet as they moved through the palm trees and out onto the sand. The sun was an ember, low to the horizon, and the sky throbbed with vibrant colours, all draining away into a band of neon pink above the horizon. They stood in silence and watched the colours change.

Out at sea the tsunami waves moved rapidly through deep ocean waters, hundreds of miles an hour, but were barely noticeable on the surface. As they reached the shallower coastal waters, though, they slowed, began to lumber, and grew.

Music from the beach bars reached them on a warm breeze. Morwenna slipped her hand out of Beverley's and reached into her bag for the bug spray. She applied it liberally across her exposed, freckled skin. The astringent chemical smell smeared with the coconut slick of her high-factor sun cream. The sun hated her but the insects loved her. Conversely, Beverley was already a walnut brown and declined the mosquito repellent with a grunt.

The evening tide was receding rapidly. Other tourists were out on the beach exploring freshly exposed rock pools. Behind them, back near the beach bars, some of the locals were shouting. Morwenna didn't understand what they were saying. They walked further out as the pink and yellow sky ripened into darker oranges and purples.

"It's beautiful," Morwenna said. "Can we make peace?"

Bev was looking out at the distant band of retreating sea as the breeze stiffened and moved the curls around her neck and ears. There was a rumble like distant thunder. Beside her Morwenna felt unmoored, far from home and drifting away from how things had been. They'd met in their final year at university, Bev crossing a busy gay bar to shout over the music: "I see you in lectures but never anywhere else. Definitely never here. Are you into girls then?" as blunt as that. By the end of the night and many drinks later they were snogging. Up until that point Morwenna had only been in one relationship, a brief, chaste affair at 16 with a boy who, in hindsight, was probably gay himself. Morwenna's own coming out (even to herself) had been a slow negotiation which only really began after she'd moved to university. Bev's arrival poured jet fuel on what had been a tentative and private process, and Morwenna gave herself up to that excitement with giddy abandon. After graduating they moved in together. Morwenna quickly landed a pretty decent job and not long after that Beverley started talking about travelling.

"Mor," Beverley said and stopped walking, "I can't do this anymore."

"Okay, we can go back." Further down the beach one of the many stray dogs of the resort started barking

"No," Bev said, "I mean I can't do *this*." She moved her hands back and forth between them.

"Don't," Morwenna said.

"I'm sorry, it's not working."

"I gave up my job so that we could go travelling."

"I never asked you to do that. I didn't want," Beverley bit her tongue.

"Didn't want what? To go travelling? You wouldn't stop going on about it."

"I didn't want to go travelling with *you*," she said. She finally said it.

That took the wind out of Morwenna. Her throat and chest tingled and she knew her skin was flushing crimson. There was more shouting on the beach but it seemed very far away. There was another noise which sounded distant and very close at the same time, like rushing blood. People were running past them now. All along the beach people were running up the shore. Some were shouting. The wind was more insistent and the roaring sound was suddenly louder, like an approaching jet engine. A Thai local some way up the beach was waving his arms and calling "Big wave! Big wave!" Nearer, an American tourist screamed "Get off the beach!" Beverley's face dropped and Morwenna turned to see the sea rushing back in; a black mass of seething water rising in front of the red sky. There were fishing boats caught in the wave, turning like flotsam. People who'd ventured further out were running towards them as the wave rose at their heels. A man stumbled and seconds later he was gone.

"Jesus, run," Beverley said, yanking Morwenna's arm. They sprinted towards the lights of the road and the hotels and restaurants. Screams sounded all around them, becoming lost in the gaining cacophony of ever-breaking thunder at their backs. Someone ran into them and sent Morwenna sprawling across the sand, gasping. Beverley paused for a moment, half turned, then began to run again. Morwenna watched in disbelief as she disappeared into the rush of people in the gathering darkness.

She left me.

The noise was unbearable now, a churning rumble so close that Morwenna felt the sand shaking beneath her hands. Cold, black water flew past her, up to her elbows, and suddenly everything grew dark as the gathering sea towered at her back.

She left me.

In that moment something at her core which had always been hot liquid suddenly ossified.

She waited for the inevitable, bone-breaking impact of water and thought it had come when all sound and motion instantly stopped. She thought her senses had been slammed from her body. But that moment stretched out – the fleeing silhouettes of people remained as statues and the absolute absence of sound pervaded. She breathed in shakily and let the air out in a slow stream. The killing wave never came. She pushed herself, shivering, onto unsteady legs. It was cold beneath the tsunami's thick umbrella of shadow. She turned and craned her neck to face the monster rearing over her but frozen in its emotionless charge.

She stood like that for some time. The broiling kinetic energy of the water was plain to see on its churned and roiling surface, but although it was bursting to overwhelm her it never advanced. The sky was a thick red, but it never got any darker. Everything was silence.

The people around her were stopped in their flight like the petrified bodies at Pompeii.

With small steps at first, eyes fixed on the wave, she backed away. She believed that if she took her eyes off the water even for a moment it would swallow her. Soon, though, she backed into a throng of bodies, toppling some, and had to turn and look where she was going. In the dim light of dusk, she picked a barefooted path through the waxwork melee of people, overturned beach chairs and parasols. She tip-toed around a tumbling fat man in a garish floral shirt; past a woman clutching a child, her face contorted in terror; a family scrambling to keep together. She moved up onto the road, the tarmac warm on the soles of her feet, and navigated the eerily still cars in motion.

Off the beach and closer to the hotels the picture was less confused. Many people were still frozen in a run, shouting, but the waves of panic had not yet reached the pools, foyers, bars, and restaurants. Morwenna padded in a daze through it all in absolute silence save for the noises she made: her footfall; her breath; the click of a dry-throated swallow.

She wanted to get back to her hotel room. It was an impulse rather than a conscious thought, the same way a child woken by a nightmare is driven to their parents' bedroom. She wanted her room and her bed, with her clothes in the drawer and Beverley telling her off for being so stupid.

Her footsteps echoed in the hotel lobby, slapping against floor tiles. The artificial light seemed to throb and made her eyes ache as she moved towards the lifts. She pressed every call button but the displays never changed and the sounds of descending lifts never came, so she moved as if sleepwalking towards the door to the stairs. It slammed behind her and sent a loud, banging echo up the hollow stairwell. It wasn't until she reached her floor and her door that she realised that she'd dropped her bag somewhere along the way and with it her key card. Still in a daze, she knocked as if expecting Beverley to answer.

She must still be out. I hope she's not too drunk when she gets back.

She leaned against the door and slid to the ground. The adrenaline which had flooded her body was souring and exhaustion claimed her. From sitting she gently collapsed onto her side and curled up in front of her hotel room door. Sleep pulled her into its own dark waters, and as she floated away the rhythm of her breathing sounded like the ocean.

No time had passed when she awoke. She took the stairs back to the ground floor and when she exited the hotel it was still dusk; the world around her was still a diorama of impending catastrophe; and although she dared not walk down onto the sand, she could still feel the halted rush of the tsunami halfway up the beach. Nothing had changed except for the hooks of hunger in her belly which drove her out into the evening.

Without a plan she headed back to the restaurant she and Beverley had visited the night before… or was it earlier that same night? As she neared the place, she moved through stationary plumes of aroma – bursts of cooking smells set like invisible jewels in the air – and her mouth filled with saliva.

The restaurant was a snapshot of bustle – waiters paused in their navigation of tables whilst diners, mid-conversation, raised forks and glasses to their mouths. In the open kitchen at the back chefs were shrouded in steam, tossing their woks, vegetables and meat flung into the air like acrobats, while flames burst and curled around the underside of their pans.

The twists of hunger began to hurt, so she sidled up to the nearest table – a middle-aged couple with a carafe of red wine and a jug of water between them and dishes she could not easily identify. She stole out a hand and snatched some rice off the lady's plate. It was still hot and it was spicy, but Morwenna shovelled more quick mouthfuls, expecting the woman to scold her at any moment. But admonishment never came.

Morwenna slid a spoon off the table and continued to eat, crouched next to the dining couple. Soon her mouth was on fire and she needed a drink. She reached for the jug of water and to her surprise found that the contents wouldn't pour. She tilted the jug then shook it, but the gelatinous water only jiggled. She dipped her spoon in and scooped out a blob of water which she slurped up like the strawberry jelly she used to eat as a child. The gooey lump of water burst like a berry in her mouth and she dug out another spoonful of drink.

She glanced over at the table she'd shared with Beverley earlier and remembered the lash of Bev's comments. That hard, brittle thing inside her chest cracked just a little, and she clamped down on it instantly. In that splinter of a second the babbled clamour of the restaurant returned – a blast of noise – and everyone moved just a fraction – and beneath that din, did she hear the approaching rush of water and distant screaming? She rocked back on her heels, scared. It seemed this stay of execution was not permanent. This frozen moment, hanging like a bauble from a Christmas tree, could be shattered.

How far inshore would the waves come?

Outside, she moved through her new twilight world until she found someone on a bike. He was a local boy, scrawny but still difficult to grapple off his seat. She half-lifted, half-pulled him from his bicycle and dragged him to the side of the road.

How far away would be safe?

She weaved a rickety path around pedestrians, cars, and tuk-tuks, picking up speed as she left the beach behind. After maybe two miles of slow climbing, she pictured the face of the boy whose bike she'd stolen. She saw him as she'd left him, on his back like a turtle, still in a seated position with his arms out to grip the handlebars. She imagined the cold, inky waves wiping him out in a blink and let the bike slow to a stop. The hard thing in her chest pushed against her sternum like a cuttlefish bone. She looked back towards the shore and saw the distant sun dipped into the sea. From here the water looked blood red as it reflected the sky and raced towards everyone below. If she left them behind it would be like murdering them. She was just as stuck as everyone else. She screamed at the implacable sea and then, after a few sobbing minutes, she turned the bike around and began pedalling back towards the beach.

Time did not pass, but Morwenna fell into her own circadian rhythm. She ate when she was hungry, stealing from plates or raiding hotel kitchens, and she slept when she was tired. After three uncomfortable sleeps in hotel corridors, she took a rock to one of the door handles (but not her own room, not that empty place with no Beverley). In between eating and sleeping she tried to clear the beach.

She moved the children first. She pulled them off the sand and out of restaurants; she pried them out of parents' arms, one by one, and carried them into her hotel, up flights of stairs to where they'd not be touched when the waves rolled in. She set about this with such determination that by the time she worried about splitting up families she'd already collected dozens of them. When the bubble burst and the waters rushed in these children and their parents would be terrorized to suddenly find themselves transported and separated. After that she tried to keep groups of people together, although moving adults was far more cumbersome and energy-sapping. She could haul maybe eight or nine adults into the hotel and up four flights of stairs before her strength gave out for that day (or what she thought of as a day).

For each person she saved she had to pass dozens of others, and it was their faces which haunted her. Worse than the ones twisted in fear were those further from the beach who were frozen in oblivious smiles and laughter, happy but no less doomed. Whenever exhaustion forced her to stop, she thought about the ones she'd left outside.

She tried cars but engines wouldn't turn over; there was no spark. No machine would work, no microwave or oven, but she found she could cook if there was already an open flame to hand. Her curious fingers had quickly discovered that the frozen flames were no less hot.

She concentrated on the area outside her own hotel at first, but after weeks in this lonely, silent tableau the enormity, the impossibility of her task slowly set in. The wave would come. It would travel a kilometre inland at least, and it would hit the whole western coast of Thailand. No matter how many people she dragged to higher ground she would have to abandon thousands more.

Some nights, when a peculiar mood took her, she would stand in front of the monster wave. Inside its shadow she regarded it solemnly; sometimes she would hold out a hand and touch its spumy surface. It was the only thing which kept her company. It wanted to be released.

"Soon," she would tell it. "Soon, but not tonight. Let me gather a few more." And then she would set about her task again, and for each face saved she tried to lower her gaze from the ones she passed by.

Her teeth began to ache and her gums bled. Her bones hurt and her muscles complained. Some nights she would sit on the roof of the hotel and stare, unblinking, into the sun. This perpetual sundown was making her sick. Her skin was sallow and she as weak. But each evening she dragged more people out from under the descending paw of the wave. She filled hotel rooms and corridors and had to begin climbing to higher floors, piling bodies one atop another.

She did this for maybe a year.

Then, one evening, she stumbled across Beverley.

She found a running body in an alley between two shops and began to grapple it, avoiding the face and grateful that it was someone lithe and light. The smell of her hair brought Morwenna out of her automata reverie. Those little dark curls.

She met Bev's brown eyes and cried out, tripped, and sent them both tangled to the floor. Morwenna thrashed and kicked to be out from under the dead weight of her girlfriend, and once free she scooted a few metres on her backside and sat and stared. A sob rose like a bubble up her throat, thick and sour. She began to shake and rose and walked away swiftly through streets of mannequins. Her breath came in jags and she felt her pulse at her temples. She was making little noises in the back of her throat and the brittle thing at her core shot out barbs like jellyfish stings. She walked, flapping her hands at her side, making loud shushing noises through her teeth with each breath until her panic subsided. Eventually, inevitably, she slunk back to the alley.

She hooked her arms under Bev's and hoisted her off the floor. Slowly, carefully, she carried her through the streets and down onto the beach. Bev's heels dragged in the sand, her body tense in Morwenna's grasp. Together they went down to the wave and Morwenna placed her onto the cold, wet sand and sat opposite her. Morwenna's face was slick with tears, her nose was snotty and she was ugly from crying. She reached a pallid hand out and stroked Beverley's tanned cheek.

"It's alright," she croaked. Her unused voice sounded like nails. Her dried lips split.

It was cold in the shadow of the tsunami. It wasn't something Morwenna could hold back forever.

There was fear in Bev's eyes and Morwenna tried to sooth her.

"You got scared, that's all. It's alright now."

She took the brittle thing inside her and broke it to pieces.

"It's alright now."

The waves came rolling in.

UPON RETURNING HOME FROM THE GREAT WAR

During the train journey north Tom Gibbs felt a strange kind of transubstantiation taking place around him. What had first been a raucous, rammed mass of demobbed men – calling and singing; smoking and joking – was slowly unpicking itself into separate bodies. With each stop more of those bodies were shed, scattered out across England, and by the time the train reached his stop at Gadsby, at around 2am, the remaining men had been gently rocked into a growing introspection.

Tom disembarked at Gadsby alone. He missed the step and tripped onto the platform, stumbling amongst the steam and hiss of the engine like a fish dropped onto a skillet.

Gadsby station was unassuming, no more than a length of platform and a ticket office which stood dark and empty. The cheers, flags, and crowds of Dover didn't seem real now that he was faced with that silent, stoic brick building. He was back, at last, in the small farming town where he'd spent his entire life, right up until the war had sent him running to join up.

Behind him the train champed, strained, and pulled away. There were still one or two floating faces at the carriage windows, ashen behind smeared glass, but he didn't turn to see them off. The ache from his wound had spread from his knee up his thigh during the long journey and he stamped his leg to try and work some life back into it. Then he slung his kit bag over his shoulder and set off for his mother and home.

The road to town was downhill and he soon fell into a steady march. Whenever he'd pictured home from the Front it had been Gadsby in spring or at Christmas, not this dead time of shadows with the wash of pearl blue moonlight over everything. His boots sounded loud and strange against the rustle of the hedgerows and the night-time sounds of the trees. Being out in the open beneath the stars made him uneasy. He wanted to roll a cigarette, but even now superstition stayed his hand for fear the red glow might summon a sniper's bullet. Something screamed in one of the fields on the other side of the hedge, a creature meeting its end at the claws of something larger and faster. He clomped on.

At the bottom of the hill the road would bear right and there would be a stile he could climb to cut across Jack Bendelow's fields. As a boy he and his friends had run through those fields with old man Bendelow roaring after them, cuffing them round the ears if he caught hold of them. If he took the shortcut, he could make good time and reach his mam. If she had his telegram she'd surely be up and waiting.

At the bend, though, he found that the stile had been replaced by twists of barbed wire. The claggy smell of the trenches still clung to his clothes and Tom was suddenly repulsed by the idea of tramping across tilled fields — soil and stone turned by plough blades; worms and beetles harrowed then folded back into the earth; bodies in the mud. He'd stick to the road. He paused, though, when he saw that the way didn't bend round to the right as he remembered but was forked instead. He frowned and took the right-hand path wearily, more eager than ever for a mother's greeting and perhaps a reheated meal prepared for his return.

The road began to rise gently. His kit bag occasionally slid from his shoulder, forcing him to hoist it back up. His forward march became ragged. The hedgerows were tall in shadow either side of the road and above him the moon kept her distance as she had over the battlefields of France. A fox called from some way off and up ahead a dark bulky shape lay at the side of the road. Tom slowed and approached with caution, crossing to the other side to maintain a little distance as he closed the gap. The shape moved, moaned, and Tom saw that it was an old man, small and gnome-like in a shabby overcoat, scarf, and gloves.

"You alright there, gaffer?" Tom said.

The old man looked up sharply, noticing him for the first time. "Wha? Who? Who's that?" he called out, "I don't have nothing on me worth stealing."

"Settle down, I'm not aiming to skin you. Just making me way home and you look like you could do with some help."

"Home you say? Help?" the old man looked at the sky as if trying to divine something from the stars. "It's too late now, I reckons. Missed it, I have. For the first time ever."

"Missed what?" Tom crossed the road with the intention of helping the man to his feet. In the opal light saw that the man's left trouser leg was folded up and pinned at the knee. He held out a hand and the old gadger reached up for it.

"Missed?" the old man said with a grunt as he was heaved upright. "The festival, of course."

"I've lived in Gadsby me whole life; ain't never heard of no festival," Tom said.

The old man leant on him, barely coming up to his chest, and assessed his face with rheumy eyes.

"Ah, I see, you're a young 'un," he said. "Not too many young chaps round here of late."

"Aye, well... I've been away, as you'll understand," Tom replied.

"And going home to Gadsby?"

"That's right."

"Call me Len," the old man said, then he regarded the stars again in the way most might check a pocket watch. "And you are?"

"Thomas. Tom."

The fox screamed again. Len sniffed, wobbling on one unsteady leg.

"It seems we're both going the same way, young Master Thomas. Perhaps you might want to give an old duffer a helping hand? If we're lucky there might still be some scran and ale to be had." Len unconsciously licked his lips and Tom's own hunger intensified

After a little fuss, shifting his kit bag to lay across his chest, Tom lifted Len onto his back, piggyback style. The old boy felt like bones through his thick coat, light as a bird's body. Once he was settled Tom resumed his march up the road at a steady pace. Len began to hum, something tuneless but jaunty, and Tom kept his head down and set one foot in front of the other.

The throbbing in his left leg grew insistent; tiredness began to pull at his limbs as if they were still heavy with the sludge of the trenches; the road continued to rise. Each time Tom looked up he anticipated a familiar landmark – a sign or a tree or a cottage he recognised – but there was only this nondescript road bordered by hedges. Len seemed to get heavier and the way harder and soon everything around them began to get darker as if the moon were steadily dimming. Tom wanted to rub at his eyes but couldn't lose his grip on the old man, so he blinked against the growing gloom and marched on.

Len's humming got louder as it got darker and soon Tom could only make out the next few paces ahead of him. Sometimes he thought that he could hear children snickering and whispering on the far side of the hedges, but then Len would jig up and down, cluck his tongue as if he were geeing a horse, and cackle at the joke. Tom's boots felt too heavy, clogged with mud. He felt that he was close to collapse.

Suddenly there was a crowd and chatter. Smiling faces cast in orange and black from firelight and shadows pressed in around them. Len wriggled and squirmed to be let down. Tom crouched and the old man slid off his back, patted him on the shoulder and whispered, "God bless you, son; God bless you."

As soon as he was on the ground Len hopped away into the crowd. Someone pushed a tankard into Tom's hand while other hands clapped him on the back. Through the crowd he caught sight of a green door and slate roof which must be the post office. Further up the high street he saw the weathervane that sat on top of the doctor's surgery, or was it the butcher's?

The dancing light from the nearby bonfire made it hard to make out details. There had been something sat on top of the flames – a Guy or some other effigy – but the fire had long since collapsed in on itself and he couldn't tell what was being burnt. Beyond the fire, at the far end of the high street, he saw a statue on a plinth where none had been when he'd left to sign up. It was a figure, one arm raised high, but through jumping orange flames he couldn't make out any more than that. People passed all around holding plates and picking at scraps with their fingers. All these people were old, Tom realised. Their lips were shiny in the firelight, slick with grease and fat from the feast.

"Best festival so far," a grinning old dear said to no one in particular, popping the slick ends of her fingers into a toothless mouth one at a time. "Best festival so far." Tom wanted to get to the far end of the high street but couldn't see a way through the yammering throng. Instead, he made roughly for the direction of the green post office door and slipped down an alleyway between two stone clad buildings.

Once he was round the back of the buildings the babble of the crowd was dimmed. He found himself in knot of high-walled alleys he didn't recognise and tried to orient himself based on the scant landmarks he thought he'd recognised on the main street.

The sound of dull drums began, slow, like the accompaniment to a firing squad, but they were all slightly out of time with one another. As Tom moved through the twisting warren of paths it sounded as if the drums were stalking him and he thought of the elderly crowds creeping through these back streets. The drums had a homemade sound to them of dried skin stretched over pots. They urged him on even though his leg was aching deep into the muscle now, turning his stride into a limp. Was that the murmur of the crowd bubbling beneath the beat? The sound of glistening tongues smacking wet lips?

He took a turn and found a way out into a crescent-shaped street which felt familiar. Yes, here was a set of stone steps he recognised – they'd bounced balls down them as boys – and he climbed, his breathing ragged by the time he got to the top. He leaned heavily on the cold metal handrail and from this vantage point he could see the bonfire some way below him, lighting up the town centre as if an incendiary had hit.

The air whipped around him, cooler up here, and it helped to clear his head. The sound of the drums below seemed to move away. He turned and made his way towards home with more certainty now. Buildings were thinning and he breathed more easily, rubbing at his thigh, craving the familiarity of the hearth, the kitchen, his old room.

At the top of the lane the solid square outline of his house stood against the night sky. No light was on, but it was late – much later than he had anticipated arriving – and his mother had surely gone to bed by now. He reached the front gate and was surprised at the relief he felt when it gave its familiar, rusty squeak. He crunched up the path, steps uneven and leg complaining. The front door was locked so he moved round to the back.

Once inside, the cool stillness of the kitchen was like a moment of peace, a brief ceasefire. He lingered in the dark space, breathing heavily, sweat cooling between his shoulder blades, alert for the creak of a floorboard from above. Finally, home. He almost called out. Best, perhaps, to let her sleep and get some rest himself. They could talk in the morning.

He took three deep gulps of water straight from the tap, then dropped himself onto a seat at the kitchen table and yanked at his laces like a crow at worms. He pulled his boots off and his feet throbbed gratefully on the chill floor tiles. Then he rose and moved with confidence through the dark house towards the stairs. His room was up there on the left. He could picture his bed, just twelve steps to climb – how many times had he counted his way up and down them in the dark to use the lavvie outside? He counted now as he ascended through blackness – two – three – as ever the creak on the sixth step – his leg was on fire now – eight – nine – was that a stirring from his mother's bedroom? – eleven – twelve. He tripped. Stumbled. There was a thirteenth step.

17 STOREYS OF DEATH & DESIRE

I never wanted this day to come, but there it was in the local newspaper: South Stoneham House was finally going to be demolished. The article inspired a queasy cocktail of nostalgia and fear in me. The past assaults you like that sometimes.

I moved to Southampton for my first year of university in the autumn of 1993. I remember the journey there in the back of my parents' car, and I can still recall the first time I saw the concrete tower block of South Stoneham house, same colour as the sky, filling the windscreen as we approached. The place would be my halls of residence for the next year.

I signed in on the ground floor, got my room key, and took the rickety lift to the third floor with my parents, burdened with bags and boxes. I vividly remember using my new key to let us all into my small room. It had a desk by the window, a low table for a kettle and mugs, a single bed, a narrow wardrobe, and a small mirror over the wash basin. My parents stayed for a little while and I christened the kettle, but eventually, inevitably, they had to leave. And just like that I had moved out of home.

I should explain that South Stoneham House was something of a Jekyll and Hyde building. Firstly, there was the striking mansion – a Grade II listed building close to the River Itchen attributed to Nicholas Hawksmoor (he of the occult London churches). Then there was our Stoneham, a 17-storey tower block connected to the mansion house, built in the Sixties to increase accommodation. And yes, it looked as grim and incongruous as that sounds, but what did I care how it looked from the outside? I was 18 years old, shy, nervous and in a strange city on my own; I had other things on my mind.

I would often sit on the windowsill in my room and watch the students below coming and going. I'm not sure how long I sat like that on my first day, but eventually my neighbour knocked and invited me to his room for a cup of coffee. My first university friend. Without that kind gesture I may well have sat alone for the rest of the day.

That first weekend we were woken in the middle of the night by the fire alarm. Stoneham's gusty concrete stairwell was open to the elements and we all tramped down in our pyjamas, dressing gowns, and anoraks. We huddled outside in the cold while the fire brigade made their obligatory checks of every floor. They knew better than we did that this was just the first of many tit-for-tat fire alarm pranks between the three student halls along that road. They must have hated us.

That same weekend us freshers were gathered for a safety talk. We were taught the best route to walk from Stoneham to the campus, taking the back streets to avoid Burgess Road and the Flowers Estate where the odd gang of locals were sometimes partial to a spot of student bashing. I wondered if we were called "freshers" because we were fresh faces or fresh meat. I recall leaving Stoneham one evening and seeing a student being helped back inside; he was clutching his nose and there was blood down his front from just such an assault. The female students were warned never to walk through the city parks at night. The hammer attacks hadn't started yet, but once they got going no one really walked alone anywhere.

There was a Freshers' Week pub crawl, which I realise now was probably a way to guide us to the student friendly pubs in the area – down the valley towards town, but never into the city centre itself. Fuck me, there were some dives back then! Clowns and Jesters; The Hobbit; Rhinos. 50p vodka shots; sawdust on sick; the sting of piss in your nostrils in the gents (unless the urinals were blocked, in which case you were paddling in the stuff). Heaving bodies five deep at the bar, shouting over thudding music for more pound-a-pints; shots; chasers.

Sorry, I'm getting off the point. I really wanted to tell you about Stoneham House and the "Stoneham Walk". I can't remember how I first heard about it but the idea stuck in my head for some reason.

Before I get to that, though, mentioning Burgess Road reminded me of something else that happened. I want to tell you about the seagull.

You see, we didn't always avoid Burgess Road. It was the quickest route to campus after all, and it was dotted with newsagents and little supermarkets. If you were late for a lecture or seminar and needed to grab something to eat it was ideal. It was a straight run up a gentle hill along a busy road and during the day it was mostly fine.

I was halfway up Burgess Road one morning and there was a small flock of about six or seven seagulls in the air. They were diving to the tarmac then hauling themselves back into the air in the gaps between oncoming cars, trying to scoop up some food which had been dropped on the road. As I got level with them one gull dived far too late, just as a lorry thundered past, and it disappeared beneath unrelenting wheels. There was no way it could have survived, but as the lorry charged on, I saw it stuck to the middle of the road, waving one wing weakly like a drowning man. The lights further down the hill had changed and the road was free of traffic for a few moments. In that lull it craned its neck to stare at what was left of its body. Its lower half was squashed red into the road, tyre marks in mince, and it snapped its beak silently at the sight.

I felt locked into that moment with this creature and couldn't bear its silent screams at the sight of its own burst body. I cast my eyes around for a brick or a stone and wondered if I could bring myself to step into the road and crush that snapping head, to bring its horror to an end. Luckily for me the lights changed again and a convoy of three quick cars did the job for me.

I was studying English Literature, by the way. I aspired to be a writer. Looking back, I was a pretentious little sod who knew nothing about the way the world worked. For the next three years that didn't matter, though, because I slowly made friends and settled into the tidewaters of university life. I was cosseted in a world of beer and literature and lectures; drinking endless coffee and cadging fags in the refectory; talking all afternoon about books, films, and my courses: Victorian Fantasy; Tragedy; Renaissance Sexualities; Death and Desire. I wrote terrible poetry and wanted to be a novelist. I found a place for myself, but I was still shy, and I was lonely, even with my new friends.

Not long after Halloween news spread across campus of a late-night attack in one of the city parks. We didn't know it at the time but that was the first of the hammer attacks. A man had been hospitalised with what the local paper euphemistically called life-changing injuries. Back at Stoneham the Vice Warden gave more safety warnings and the girls were given personal attack alarms, but we still fell out of pubs and clubs and staggered home through lonely streets, spilling cones of chips on the way back to our implacable tower.

I smoked weed for the first time. I got it into my head that if I was going to be a writer then I ought to try something hallucinogenic at least once; the works of Coleridge, Shelley and Blake demanded it! With that in mind I took the rattling lift to the 13th floor and visited the kid who sold us our weed.

I'd never travelled that high up the tower before and was surprised when the lift doors opened to a blast of strong wind. The wind always seemed to race around the upper reaches of the Stoneham, restlessly snaking up and down the stairwell.

The very top floor, the 17th, was off limits. I think it held the lift machinery.

Below that the 16th floor was a sort of observation deck, glassed off with a panoramic view of the city.

From the 15th floor down, though, each landing formed an echoey sort of balcony which had reinforced glass in its middle section but was open to the elements on either side. I always worried those gaps might invite suicide. They also felt like a challenge, a dare to do the Stoneham Walk – to climb to the 15th floor, step out through one of those gaps, work your way across the front of the building, and climb back in at the far end. The idea haunted me.

All the rooms in the place had the same layout, so our dealer's room felt uncannily familiar. It smelt of incense sticks and deodorant and the quality of light at this height was subtly different to my own room.

Unsurprisingly, he was more than happy to sort me out. I was still wary, I'd never done anything like that before, but he told me about a house party he was going to that weekend. He suggested I tag along and that way he could keep an eye on me while I dropped the acid. The idea of being in a house full of strangers was my idea of social hell, but I wanted this experience, so I agreed.

He was good to his word. At the party I was awkward and didn't know how to speak to any of these people who seemed effortlessly cool, but he did look after me. He gave me a microdot and when I came up he guided me to the chill out room, sat me in a corner, and checked on me every now and again whilst I quietly went about the business of tripping my balls off.

I won't bore you with the details of my experience, but I'd done it; I had followed in the footsteps of The Romantic Poets. I was going to be a writer.

At some point I left the party, my mind humming, and followed a very circuitous route home using the distant dark rectangle of Stoneham as my North Star. Back on the third floor my mates were still up so I sat with them and drank beer and waited for the walls to stop breathing.

The next morning the news was all over campus: a woman had been attacked and killed that night. University life continued.

I had trouble sleeping after that. One night, after everyone on my floor was asleep, I heard the fire door at the end of our corridor bang open and the soft shuffle of someone making their way from door to door. I assumed it was a drunk student who had taken the lift to the wrong floor and was looking for their room. The closer they got, though, the clearer I heard a dull slap like a bare foot or the palm of a hand against the floor. The corridor and stairwell lights were on all night, so there was always a bar of yellow light beneath my door after dark. Now a shadow moved across that light. It stayed there, swaying for long seconds while I held a hand over my mouth and tried not to make a sound. Eventually the shadow moved back the way it had come, and those fleshy slapping sounds receded until I heard the bang of the fire door once more.

I wish I could say that only happened the once, but those night-time visits continued and became more frequent.

My days were a brew of learning and longing. Shyness can be crippling and I wore a sarcastic kind of wit like armour. I pined after beautiful girls and dove into texts as an escape – Satan's fall in *Paradise Lost*; Latimer's vision of his own death in *The Lifted Veil*; a stage strewn with body parts in *Titus Andronicus* while elsewhere body parts were sewn back together in *Frankenstein*, wherein the creature read *Paradise Lost,* and Satan fell all over again. I studied Freud's theory of the death drive, and in the works of Poe I saw death and desire become interchangeable, and all the time my own solitary sadness grew.

I had my friends, of course; we had good times. One night at Stoneham a mate and I serenaded the people below from the third-floor balcony with a full-throated, drunken rendition of "Something's Gotten Hold of My Heart". He stood at the right-hand gap singing Marc Almond's part while I was on the left giving my best Gene Pitney.

There were other times when I found myself standing on the 15th floor at night, looking out over the rooftops. The wind stalked up there; fire doors slammed and voices echoed around the hollow space from lower floors; the lift clattered, and the ping of its opening doors reached me, but no one ever spilled out onto the floor where I lurked.

Somewhere down below a man full of cold rage walked the streets with a hammer hidden in his coat, his knuckles white around the handle. By then he had attacked five people.

I went back to Crowthorne for Christmas and slept in my old bedroom. I caught up with school friends but kept expecting to see faces from my university life walking those quiet village roads. And whenever I looked up, stumbling home from the pub, usually thinking about a girl, I expected to see the top floors of Stoneham House looming over the treetops.

Things got a bit ragged. My attendance dropped. I missed a couple of essay deadlines. It was no certain thing that I'd get the grades to make it to the second year of the course.

One evening I was working late in the Hartley Library on campus making hurried, last-minute notes on Aeschylus' *The Eumenides*. The essay was due the next day and I'd have to stay up all night writing it. The hush of that place always felt a little erotic to me – speaking *sotto voce*; the scratch of pens on paper; people shifting in their seats and moving quietly through the book stacks.

It was near closing time and the study area around me was emptying save for a girl who shared some of my seminars. Once I'd noticed her, I couldn't concentrate on the books in front of me. Instead, I watched her as she diligently took notes, pushed her hair behind her ears and tapped her foot unconsciously, wishing I had the nerve to walk over and strike up a conversation. Any attempt at small talk on my part would be awkward and stumbling. I felt the sear of embarrassment at just the thought of it. She didn't want me bothering her while she was working, so I gathered up my books to return them to their shelves, dejected.

In amongst the stacks the smell of old pages was strong. My movement through the rows turned on overhead spotlights as I slotted books back where they belonged. It was already dark outside and it occurred to me that I could offer to walk back to halls with her; no one wanted to make journeys like that alone anymore. I might not sound too clumsy suggesting something like that.

As I replaced my final book, I became aware of irregular breathing on the other side of the stack. Someone was there, standing motionless. They sounded as if they were breathing through a slack, open mouth. That neighbouring row was unlit, though. Whoever was there must have been standing still for some time for the overhead light to have timed out.

There was a slight wheeze and then a wet sound – not like swallowing, but the *attempt* of a swallow. If I moved the slanted books in front of me then I could see who was there, and even though part of me didn't want to know, I slid my fingertips between two thick volumes. At that moment the alarm sounded – fifteen minutes till the library closed – and I withdrew my hand and left the oppressive rows, head down and in a hurry.

Back at my desk I gathered up my notes and pens and stuffed them into my backpack. The girl from my seminars was gone. I made for the stairs and hastened down and round, expecting at any moment to hear a door slamming open above me and then the cold slap of skin on the stairs.

I walked home in double time through the back streets and barrelled into Stoneham as if I were any safer inside. I stayed up all night drinking coffee and tried to turn my scratchy notes into a passable essay. Right through till dawn, while I tapped away on an old PC, I kept my ears open for the sound of the fire doors at the end of the corridor and the shambling gait of my nocturnal visitor.

A couple of days later I got a note to see one of my lecturers. We sat in his book-lined office and he held the ragged print out of the last-minute essay I'd crammed into his pigeonhole.

"I think maybe your essay got saved together with bits of something else you were working on?" he said, almost apologetically. I didn't know what he was talking about and took the crumpled pages when he held them out. The essay was something I'd cobbled together about the Furies in Greek literature.

"It's your footnotes," he said, and I scanned the bottom of each page. Where the footnotes should have cited the sources of my quotes, they all said:

Why does she come silent to my door every night?

I flushed and became flustered. I think he was embarrassed on my behalf. He gave me till the end of the week to "sort the bugs out" and I left as quickly as I could.

Things seemed to move quite fast after that. I'd light a cigarette and realise that I hadn't finished the one which was already in my hand. I drank too much. On nights out my laughter was a little too loud. Most nights I couldn't sleep and that lost person would lurch through the fire door at the end of the corridor and stumble up to my room and rock back and forth.

The attacks were becoming more frequent. Two people were hospitalised on the same night in January. One died.

It was February when I eventually climbed to the 15th floor to complete the Stoneham Walk.

Stoneham House was throwing a Valentine's Ball and the ground floor was heaving with students from all three halls. Even up as high as I was, I could hear the faint bass from the dancefloor.

I stood to the left of the balcony, unsteady and very drunk. The concrete reached up to my waist and beyond that there was only night air. I grabbed the frame of the central section of reinforced glass and pulled myself up. It was a fine night, standing in that gap with 15 storeys of space between me and the concrete floor below. Up there the air constantly hit the building and slid around and through its draughty ribs. It was chilly and calm compared to the sweaty, heaving crowds and music downstairs. I gripped the cold metal window frame and swayed, taking deep breaths. I expected to hear calls from down below, shrieks of surprise or panic, but no one looked up and no one saw me in that black rectangle of shadow.

I swung out and around the window frame and planted my left foot on the window ledge outside. I kept a grip on the frame with my right hand, white-knuckled, and faced back onto the landing through thick, smeared glass like the bottom of a bottle. I slid my left foot out a little further and carefully began to tilt my weight across and onto it. Then, with my face pressed against the windowpane and my breath steaming the glass, I brought my right foot out to meet it.

I sent my left hand searching, flat against the glass, but there were no handholds. With my breath coming faster I sent my left foot out again, stealing inches across the lip of the ledge. Again, I shifted my weight to the left and slowly pulled my right foot beneath me. Then I sent my left foot scuffing out once again. I could hear the sole of my trainer scraping across the pockmarked concrete of the ledge, and through those thin soles I could feel the edge against the heel of my foot. I became acutely aware of the gulf of space at my back as the wind ruffled my untucked shirt, sending it flapping like a bird wanting to take flight. I took another sliding step to the left.

I was halfway across the face of the building when I saw the silent figure on the staircase, blurred and ill-defined through mottled glass. She watched from the steps between the floors then climbed one step towards me. That was when I heard the smack of her bare foot on the cold concrete step.

My legs began to shake. I pushed my left foot out further than I had before. I wanted to get inside quickly but in my rush I almost placed both hands too firmly on the glass; I nearly pushed myself backwards and out into the night void behind me.

She took another unsteady step, stumbled, and fell forwards, her left hand smacking the top step.

I tried to steady my breathing and to concentrate on moving my feet one at a time across the ledge towards the gap to my left. My fingers were almost at the window frame, but if I moved too fast I knew I'd lose my balance. I pulled my trailing right foot behind me, breathing shallowly, then I toed my left foot out. The wind raced around the building and my calf muscles started to cramp. The sudden squirt of adrenaline made my legs shake. I just needed them to hold me up for two more steps.

Again, there came the dull sound of another step towards me. I didn't want to look. I knew that if I turned and her face was on the other side of the glass, then I'd shrink back from her and fall. My cheek was pressed to the dirty glass; stabs of breath in and out through my nose; my left foot scuffed its way along the ledge.

Finally, thankfully, my fingertips met the chill frame to the left of me. I took another small step and curled my fingers around that metal bar. One more step and I would be able to grip it tighter. And for those last two steps I was certain that I would feel her questing fingers come to pry my grip loose.

I tumbled back inside and crumpled to the floor. With my back against the firm wall and my legs pulled up to my chest I kept my eyes fixed on the stairs. I could hear the distant beat of the music once again. I began to hyperventilate; I was crying and babbling. She wasn't there anymore.

Eventually, I was able to descend those 15 floors on shaky legs. I had to take the stairs; I didn't want to feel the drop of the lift. I re-joined the party. The noise, light and heat shook me back down to earth. I stumbled into my friends and told them, wild-eyed, what I'd done. I'd completed the Stoneham Walk. They asked me what the Stoneham Walk was. They didn't know what I was talking about. I began to laugh manically and couldn't stop.

For the second and third year of my degree my friends and I moved into a succession of rented houses and I had no reason to return to South Stoneham House. The random hammer attacks stopped after that first year. There had been seven attacks in total. Does someone like that ever just stop? I believe he moved away, or more likely got imprisoned for something else. Maybe he died. Maybe he killed himself.

The year after my graduation they stuck a wooden collar around the base of Stoneham tower to stop crumbling concrete falling on anyone. It was another 12 years before the place was deemed unsafe for use and emptied, but it's still standing there today, a huge white elephant. It's encased in scaffolding now, like a leg held together in a frame of pins and wires. It's wrapped in a plastic mesh, presumably because of the crumbling concrete.

I read an article which said that it cost the university £100,000 a year just to keep it like that. It was too expensive to dismantle manually and it couldn't be brought down with charges because of its proximity to the listed building it grew from, like an inoperable goitre. I kept my distance, but I kept tabs on the place. And now it's finally coming down and I'm terrified. There's something I didn't tell you. Something I've been too scared to tell anyone.

The night that I went to the house party – the night I dropped acid – something happened on the way home. My pupils were like saucers as I made my way back to Stoneham. The night was so vibrant with colour and detail, I wandered up and down streets following my fascinations, constantly distracted but trying to reach the tower. For long periods I just stood and stared at silly things which absorbed me.

Somewhere along the way I bumped into a man as he left an alleyway. He clipped my shoulder as he rounded the corner and we looked at one another for a moment. He was wearing an anorak with the hood up – the kind which zipped up into a fur-lined funnel. It seemed to my dilated eyes that there was nothing inside, just a void. And then he was gone and I heard sounds coming from the alleyway – struggled breathing – a wheezing sound.

The alley seemed to undulate like a languorous snake; straight lines refused to remain fixed. There was a shape on the ground, a bundle, and I moved towards it.

It was a person. A woman. She was on her back and was smacking one palm weakly against the ground. The air seemed to ripple with each slap. She only had one shoe on. Her bare foot was twitching. Her breathing became wet as I crouched beside her, unblinking, unsure of what I was seeing. There was a dark dent in her forehead and the eye beneath was bulging out. A blood bubble grew from one of her nostrils.

In my spangled state I reached out to try to – I don't know – I don't know what I was trying to do.

Her bare foot began to shake violently and a gurgling noise began in the back of her throat. I reached out my hand and held it over her mouth and nose. I kept it there until she stopped shaking. It wasn't long.

This morning I read that the city council has finally approved the demolition of South Stoneham Tower. What I don't know is whether she stayed there after I moved out. I don't know if she's been stumbling and crawling up and down those stairs all these years. If the dead slap of her hand and foot has been echoing through those corridors. And if she did stay there, walking the crumbling and decrepit hallways, was she looking for me? And if she was, where will she go once the tower comes down?

ACKNOWLEDGEMENTS

To pull off any great crime an aspiring villain must have means, motive, and opportunity. These are mine.

Hannah, my loving and supportive wife, provided the means. Her unwavering belief and support eventually brought me round to the idea that I could try and write again, having given up on that dream many years ago.

My motive – or at least motivation – was immeasurably aided by the support, feedback, and time of those who generously agreed to read my various works in progress:

Liane Jackson; Libby Harris; Louise Lightfoot; Emma Pope; Paul Childs; Susan Earlam and Jane Roberts-Morpeth. Thank you all.

Thanks also to Andy Murry at Comma Press for his invaluable horror short story writing course.

But the best laid plans of any criminal endeavour will come to naught without opportunity, and for that I am eternally grateful to the magnificent Regina Saint Claire, author and editor of *Local Haunts: A Horrortube Anthology*.

Without her call for submissions, I would never have written Crowthorne – my first story to see print – or any of the stories herein.

If you're still reading, you have my gratitude! And if you have enjoyed any of these tales of death and desire, I would beg your indulgence one last time and ask that you consider leaving an honest review.

Printed in Great Britain
by Amazon